# PRAISE FOR *THE HYPOTHESIS*

"In his elegantly crafted and touching debut novel, David R. Roth uses three points of view to walk us through the lives of a long-married couple facing death and their younger neighbor, who is drawn into their heavily weighted world as a bug is drawn into a spider's web. Roth effectively plumbs both the intimacy of a long marriage and its sinister potential, moving us gently toward his startling conclusion."

—Janet Benton, author of *Lilli De Jong*

"If you love reading, and especially if you've been yearning to remember why you love reading, don't miss *The Femme Fatale Hypothesis*. Here we're given, finally, a contemporary debut novel free of sanctimony, bravely alive with humanizing complexity, aswirl with genuine feeling rather than sentimentalism, indelible in its themes and images, and generously engrossing in its plot. It's all here. Your readerly mind and heart will overflow with gratitude to David R. Roth."

—M. Allen Cunningham, author of *Q&A*, *Perpetua's Kin*, and *The Green Age of Asher Witherow*

"*The Femme Fatale Hypothesis* is an expertly tuned and suspenseful story crafted with great intelligence and skill, a slow-burn book that moves deftly to its incendiary ending. Roth is a careful craftsman and a bold provocateur."

—Keija Parssinen, author of *The Ruins of Us* and *The Unraveling of Mercy Louis*

"A perfect story beautifully written. The thoughtful interplay between husband, wife, and neighbor hides secret inner worlds. The tension between what people say and what they keep private builds into a heartbreaking and wonderful drama. David Roth reminds us the minutia of everyday life is never inconsequential."

—Terese Brasen, author of *Kama*

"David Roth delivers a crushing love story involving two captivating characters, a science professor and a psychologist, married nearly fifty years, grappling with an ambiguous line between euthanasia and murder. A widow neighbor forms a dramatic triangle with her caretaking, empathy, and sexual tension. Roth is masterful at weaving science, philosophy, and literature throughout to raise life's essential questions in this thoroughly gripping novel."

—Jeffrey Greene, author of *French Spirits*

"A luminously written and impeccably well-crafted novel that explores the deepest human mysteries: love and death. In David R. Roth's suburban Marrsville, eccentric Kelsey, cold-eyed Rose and tenderhearted June form a captivating trio, three uniquely compelling characters who lead the reader on a journey that culminates in a stunning and cathartic climax. The interplay of ordinary chores and extraordinary insights, science and religion, morality and mortality, is rendered with exquisite sensitivity and startling humor. *The Femme Fatale Hypothesis* has a profound resonance in this time when we are all contemplating life's ultimate questions."

—Jake Lamar, author of *Bourgeois Blues* and *Rendezvous Eighteenth*

"David Roth brings a scientist's sensibility and toolbox to his storytelling, and his are rare instruments. He has a preternatural ability to trap moments in characters' lives and preserve them in words that amplify and crystalize human emotion. There are so many sentences in this book to be dissected, admired and marveled at. The sum total is a story that feels both self-evident and astonishing."

—Nomi Eve, author of *Henna House* and *The Family Orchard*, a Book-of-the-Month Club main selection

"Roth's radiant debut novel explores love and loss in this thoughtful meditation on what it means to be alive—and to die."

—Alison Wellford, author of *Indolence*

"David Roth's *The Femme Fatale Hypothesis* feels like the antidote for a culture numbed by excess, clamor, and shock-value. Here is a story that offers a necessary, yet understated, grace; that pulls quietly at a new sole-string with every turn. Here is writing informed by an archeology as human as it is humane. Add to that a dose of humor that is playful, witty, occasionally life-saving. The scientific turn is multi-dexterous. Expect to hear a good deal more from this level-hearted writer."

—Robert Antoni, author of *As Flies to Whatless Boys*, recognized with a Guggenheim Fellowship, and *Cut Guavas*

"In David Roth's evocative novel, *The Femme Fatale Hypothesis*, Rose Geddes is dying and yet the story is not about death but life. Recruiting their neighbor, June, to bear witness, Rose and her husband, Kelsey, sail toward the inevitable on a calm sea of habits and schedules even though love, regret, and desire still roil beneath the surface. Throughout, Roth's prose is both assured and haunting, the ink of a poet in the pen of a novelist. It is a small book in size, but the author is a big talent."

—Steven Mayfield, award-winning author of *Treasure of the Blue Whale* and the upcoming *Delphic Oracle U.S.A.*

"David Roth's *The Femme Fatale Hypothesis* is a moving contemplation of the storms and passions of aging, often overlooked by a culture that worships youth. Within the simple architecture of suburban neighbors (a widow on one side, a husband and his dying wife on the other), Roth crafts a tale of Shakespearean depth and drama while delving into the mysteries of free will and the limits of love. Roth's characters are richly drawn, utterly recognizable yet full of surprises."

—Rebecca Baum, author of *Lifelike Creatures*

# THE FEMME FATALE
# HYPOTHESIS

David R. Roth

Regal House Publishing

Published by
Regal House Publishing, LLC
Raleigh, NC 27587
All rights reserved

ISBN -13 (paperback): 9781646031764
ISBN -13 (epub): 9781646031771
Library of Congress Control Number: 9781646031764

Interior and cover design by Lafayette & Greene
Cover design © by C.B. Royal
cover image by TPYXA Illustration/Shutterstock

Regal House Publishing, LLC
https://regalhousepublishing.com

Printed in the United States of America

For my sister Etta, who taught me how to live.

And my mother, Ursula Reynolds Roth,

who taught me how to die.

"This is the first demonstration of the Femme Fatale hypothesis and also only one of very few examples of intraspecific sexual deception in the animal world. My guess is that this is a short-term strategy to try and get an easy meal."

Dr. Kate Barry
Biological Sciences
Macquarie University
Australia

# SCARSVILLE

*Monday, March 2*

The noontime chime of the church bell startles her. It scatters a thought she's been working through in recent weeks. Or more a feeling really, one of being free of Earth's tethers, of weightlessly floating and being buffeted by tiny bursts of energy. A burst for movement, another in search of stillness, of a place where she could see the world outside of its influence, its gravity, its tides; a place, she imagines, that would be far away from Marrsville.

Sitting on her front porch swing, watching the birds and squirrels fight over her freshly stocked feeder, listening to the last of the twelve tolls dissolve back to silence, June Danhill is unsettlingly aware that this isn't the same Marrsville where she and Doug grew up, married, and raised their son. No more family-owned ice cream parlor with its full-fat flavors, or cluttered book store with its Kids' Korner reading area, or Dunbar's Hobby Shop with its magnificent sailing ship model kits and a slot car track in the basement. Kevin loved to race his slot cars. Even the community pool, where Kevin set the local twenty five-meter butterfly record that stood for eight years, is gone. Protected from the river by a thirty-foot dike, the pool didn't have flood insurance. When superstorm waters destroyed the complex, the town didn't have any choice but to tear down the pump house and the shower rooms, dig up the basketball court where Kevin and his friends played tennis-ball baseball, bulldoze the rubble into the pool where June and Doug swam laps during evening adult swim hours, and top it all with fill dirt. Another piece of Marrsville's heart broken and buried. *Scarsville,* Doug had called it. *The only quaint-less town on the Delaware River. All smoke shops, nail salons, payday loan outlets, and chain pizza parlors.*

After Doug died, her decision to stay was more about the home they had created than any loyalty to the depleted town. Leaving would have been to lose Doug all over again. And Kevin had enjoyed coming home during school breaks, visiting childhood friends, keeping up little family rituals, like going to the tree farm to cut their own Christmas tree. Kevin met Bonnie while working a summer job at the mall a few miles away. They were married in the same church as June and Doug; the church whose bells startled her moments ago. Kevin and Bonnie moved into a condo across town. Their twins were born at the local hospital. Watching the crawling twins stalk her stoical Himalayan cat made the house feel like a home again.

When Kevin moved his family to California six months ago, June experienced her first untethering. For a few weeks, the weightlessness felt like a form of freedom from worldly matters, like preparing Sunday dinners that accommodated her daughter-in-law's veganism, or being available for weekly babysitting requests. She was free to travel with her birding group. She could put in more hours at the church food pantry and had more time for her garden. She joined a yoga studio and took classes whenever she wanted. But the freedom became something else when grieving and longing set in: the grieving for all that was lost; the longing to know what was left. *I should leave, too*, she catches herself thinking. *There's nothing here for me but a past.*

Her brooding is again interrupted, this time by a nerve-rattling grating coming from her neighbor's gravel driveway. Professor Geddes is pulling a garbage can behind him, shuffling his feet to avoid walking out of his house slippers. His hair needs a comb and his sweatshirt looks to be inside out and backwards. He stops when he notices June.

"Good afternoon, Mrs. Danhill."

The tone of his greeting makes her think of the way he must have addressed his former students from the lectern. More like a pronouncement of truth than a nicety.

"Good afternoon, Professor."

"I haven't missed the collectors, have I?"

"No, but I think I can hear them over on Walnut."

"Nick of time," he says. He resumes his trudge, then stops again. Twisting just his neck slightly back toward her, he adds, "Odd phrase, don't you think? How does one nick time? Or stitch it for that matter. Or is the stitch in the nick?"

June laughs courteously. "I don't know," she replies, thinking the professor is making conversation, but he is already rumbling away like an old workhorse.

He deposits his can at the curb and on the way back says, "Seventy degrees in early March. A sure sign of the apocalypse."

June mocks exaggerated concern. "I hope not."

With a smug smile that she again sees as an affectation more appropriate for the classroom, Professor Geddes says, "Yes, let's hope those bothersome climate scientists have it wrong. If they can't get tomorrow's weather right, how can we expect them to predict our doom?"

Before he can shuffle away, June asks a question that she has been meaning to ask for months. "How's Rose?"

The question seems to stump the professor. Not the question, but the fact that she has asked it. Less than ten feet of grass, a holly bush, some boxwoods, and a couple of substantial trees separate June's house from the Geddes's, and yet this is the first time she has spoken to either the professor or Rose all winter. He looks a bit more stooped and disheveled than usual. She assumes tending to Rose is taking a toll. It was late summer, right about the time Kevin moved, when the professor told her how sick Rose was. He brought it up in casual conversation, no more urgency than the weather. As he told her about the oxygen tank and Rose's difficulty getting around, it dawned on June how long it had been since she had seen Rose outside. Rose had always been an active gardener, even after her diagnosis. June had excused Rose's summer neglect of her flower beds as being due to the greater than usual heat and humidity. She's at least seventy, June guesses, and made much older by the cancer. The miserable weather had kept June inside, too, at least through early September. As she flips back through the months, she recalls the professor keeping up with the fall clean up, but Rose never reappeared. *Why haven't I thought to ask after her until now? It's embarrassingly ungenerous of me and speaks to how selfish and self-pitying I've become. True, we aren't close. We've never shared interests or even belonged to the same church. But she is my neighbor. Has been for over twenty years. And by the look of him, the professor must be having a rough go.*

After careful consideration, the professor says, "Surprisingly well. She's a tough old bird."

"Please tell her I'm thinking of her." June stops short of saying she's praying for Rose, though she did when she'd first heard. And she will again now that she's been reminded.

"Will do," the professor says, and waves over his shoulder as he continues down his driveway.

*I should offer to help,* June thinks.

The feeder rattles. A squirrel has made the leap from an overhanging branch. Two house sparrows abandon the swaying column of seed and tsk their disapproval from the quince.

Kelsey Geddes loads the bed tray as if preparing a gift. Despite all the little details that are dropping from memory like leaves from winterizing branches, one kernel of knowledge will follow him to his grave: For Rose, presentation is an obsession. Not in a bad way. There is nothing prim about her. Quite the contrary. She simply sees beauty in balance, life's tits and tats. He remembers this because he has always respected it. Nature, he knows, has a way of evening scores, of seeking homeostasis. It is why he centers the bowl of potato-leek soup, places the tumbler of iceless sparkling water upper right, and arranges the board of warm, sliced baguette, softened wedge of taleggio. *Or is it asiago. No, taleggio.* And a small pot of olive tapenade on the left. He sets the spoon and cheese knife on the paisley napkin just to the right of the soup. The antique etched bud vase holding its single red grocery store rose is in the upper left. He steps back to assess his work as she will, with an admiring, critical eye. He moves the cheese knife from the napkin to the cheese board, turns the bud vase so the nod of the flower will be toward her. Details. He imagines her approval. *Look what you've done*, she'll say.

He extends his right hand under the tray to support the weight; his left thumb secures the base of the vase. He pauses for a moment to let the slight tremor in his left-hand pass. *That's it. Pay attention now. No rush.* He silently rehearses his opening line. He navigates the abandoned dining room with practiced precision, checks his grip before starting up the switchback staircase, and moves confidently down the hallway to the bedroom where his exquisite Rose wilts.

"Luncheon is served," he announces, giving it his best Downton Abbey head-butler basso.

Rose, already propped up in the rented hospital bed with her arms outside the covers and fingers laced in her lap, opens her eyes and manages a thin smile. *A good sign*, he thinks.

"Look what you've done. The flower's—nice touch," she says.

Her labored staccato speech still sometimes takes Kelsey by surprise. He nudges her oxygen tank with his leg and maneuvers to place the tray across her lap. "It's a bit early," he says, "but winter's gloom has lingered long enough. It's seventy degrees outside. I thought we could use a bit of spring in here."

She extends her blue-gray hand to him. He takes it in both of his. Hers is winter made flesh. He warms it between his palms. They hold this therapeutic embrace for a long moment. He gently rubs his hands back and forth. She holds her gaze on his face. He looks at her hands. As difficult as it is to witness what the illness has done to her flesh, its dulling effect on her once-glistening ice-blue eyes is many times worse.

"Thank you, Kel," she says, drawing her hands away so he'll look up.

"It's nothing, love. Peasant fare. No effort at all."

"It's everything—to me," she huffs.

"None of that now."

"None of what?"

"Maudlinism."

"I can't thank you—without being maudlin?"

"Of course, you can. I'm being silly."

"You're not eating?" she asks.

"I ate while you were sleeping."

"What will you do—this afternoon?"

"With any luck, write."

"How's it going?"

"Slow to start, I'm afraid." He looks at his hands as if the difficulty is with his fingers.

"It'll come," she says, with as much reassurance as she can muster. She puts her hand on his. "All work and no play…"

"Yes, well, this Jack is a bit of a bore I'm afraid."

Rose points at the clothing tag dangling from his collar. "Your sweatshirt."

"What?"

"Inside out."

"So it is."

"And backwards."

"I must have a really good reason for that."

Rose grins. "No doubt."

He moves her desk bell from the bedside table to her lunch tray and stands to leave. "Ring when you need me."

"Good luck," she says, tucking the napkin under her chin.

Kelsey catches himself on the way out. "Oh, I almost forgot. Our neighbor, Mrs. Danhill, she says hello."

"Does she?" Rose says. "Next time tell her—deliver the message herself. Your hellos sound—too much like goodbyes."

He smiles and lingers to watch her manage her first bite. Her mouth opens like a baby bird's as her hand trembles the spoon to her lips. *These are the moments we have left.*

Rose sets the spoon down and turns to the photograph of her father that keeps her company on the bedside table. She speaks silently, breathlessly, effortlessly. *It won't be long now. I can feel it. Death is unmistakable, isn't it? But it's not the same for me. 'The pale guy's pale pony is getting restless,' you said, like death was outside looking*

*in. It's not like that for me. It's more like I've been running a long race and have hit the wall. That little voice that used to say come on, you can do it, is saying what the fuck are you doing? Not helpful, that voice.*

She looks at the omniscient picture, waits for his response. Her eighty-year-old father, nearly a decade before a stroke would put him flat on his back, is posed on his skis at the top of a black-diamond run, poles planted as if he's ready to launch, smiling at the camera and gritting a lit cigarette. *Please don't be too eager for me to join you. I know it's selfish. I just want to wring a little more time out of this old dishrag of a body. I've earned my selfishness. Married forty-seven years in less than four months. Can you believe it? What was your longest? Eight, maybe ten years. And I've been pretty good company up until these last couple, if I do say so myself. Which is a good deal more than your women would say about you.*

Forty-seven years. If asked how she and Kel did it, she'd struggle to come up with an answer that anyone would understand. Why do any animals mate for life? Because some bundle of brain cells says so? An act of nature-defying will? Could it be love? Laziness? Fear? What's the secret to staying together forty-seven years? Not leaving.

Rose still marvels at how they survived their grad school years in Oklahoma. Kel was something new to her back then. Child-like and loyal as a therapy horse. At twenty-five, still a giddy kid fascinated by bugs, Kel followed her to OU from UC. Rose is convinced he hated the plains more than she did, if that was possible. But he never complained. When she did, he would say something sappy about their personal Norman Conquest. It made her want to smack him and marry him, in that order.

Rose isn't sure she ever said it out loud—maybe once to her friend Maggie decades later after at least two bottles of wine—but she believes coming east saved their marriage. Her father never believed her when she told him how much she loved it here. It's not the Big Sky or Colorado's breath-stealing Rockies. But coming off those plains years, the rolling, torna-do-free hills of Pennsylvania were like a down comforter. She could stand outside and not see a horizon. The hills and trees all point up, like you're lying down and the world is cuddling up to you. She feels like she's in the world rather than on it. Her father wouldn't have been able to stand all the people. She admits there have been plenty who taxed her limited store of patience over the years. But the move was good for her and Kel. It kept them close. A couple of co-dependent loners tucked away in a sylvan suburbia...*two solitudes that meet, protect, and greet each other.* Rilke had it just right.

*And I still love it here. And he still needs me. I know, I know. You think he's always needed me too much. Wean that pup, you'd say. He was what, fifty? Ha, you're such an asshole. You, who never needed anyone. What you could never understand is I love Kel's need. And that's not selfish. 'Love seeketh not itself to please, nor for itself hath any care, but for another gives its ease.' The irony is not lost on me that you introduced me to Blake. Not that you were any good at his divine love. But you were great at talking about it. That must've been how you won your women. We can't resist a silver tongue attached to a rattlesnake heart.*

She remembers the pep talk he gave her on his porch in Steamboat Springs. She had told him she wasn't sure she wanted to go back to Oklahoma after spring break. He hadn't tried to talk her into returning. Not directly. Sitting on his deck— chatting about life's little quirks, about the arrogance of fretting over petty human woes while a billion or so tiny lights, some of them entire galaxies, stared down at them—her father had said, "A body is better for loving and being loved." Then he'd said— and this is why she remembers—he'd said, "But the love has to be true. Not true love. Love that's true. Like that sky." She had looked up and nodded, though not exactly sure what he was getting at because so much of what came out of his mouth was bullshit. But, of course, he was right. She knows it now.

*Damn if loving Kel hasn't made me better. Both of us. Not to say there wasn't...isn't plenty of room for improvement.*

Rose stops to consider what she's said. She knows it's not really what she means when she talks about Kel needing her. As sweet as it is to think of theirs as a love story, he needs her now because he's not all he was. He'll never admit it, but she sees it. He's keeping it together for her. Trying to squeeze as much spark as possible out of every neuron so she'll think he'll be just fine after she's gone. But the old gray matter ain't what it used to be. Sometimes she looks into his eyes and it's like she's seeing all the way to the back of his skull, an endless, threshed Oklahoma wheat field converging with a cloudless sky.

She returns to her father's beckoning gaze. *Please don't look at me like that. I don't have a kid to help me die. I'm on my own here. I'm not like you. Being still doesn't torture me. This isn't the misery for me that it was for you. And Kel's trying so hard. Honestly, I didn't think the crazy old bug man had it in him, but look at this asiago, tapenade, and warm bread…my god. There's more to him than nearly fifty years could reveal. And now so much less. I can't go yet. What would he do without me?*

⤫

Kelsey reads through his opening again. Not so long ago, writing was a process of discovery. The thoughts tumbled out like atoms and assembled themselves into their natural molecular shapes, covalently compounding themselves in what felt like effortless alchemy. When did it become such work, effort that demands exhausting persistence? He feels like a Boy Scout trying to start his first hand-drill fire. He keeps reading and rereading in an effort to remember what he was thinking when he wrote the words in the first place.

THE RIDDLE OF THE FEMME FATALE HYPOTHESIS
*Sexual Deception and Defenses in a Cannibalistic Mating System*
*K. A. Geddes, PhD Professor Emeritus, University of Pennsylvania*

INTRODUCTION

*She is dying to eat; he must die so she may eat. Why?*

*What possible advantage could a species enjoy by evolving a reproduction-specific signaling system that provides a physiological advantage to dying females over more robust ones when it comes to attracting a mate? The obvious answer is none. A less fit, less fecund female has less chance of producing adequate and healthy offspring and ipso facto puts the species at a procreative disadvantage.*

*Yet Australian biologist Kate L. Barry has published the results of the first empirical study to provide evidence of sexual deception, via sophisticated chemical cues no less, that appears to prioritize the survival of the individual over that of the species—the first demonstration of the Femme Fatale hypothesis.*

*Dr. Barry's study demonstrated that a female false garden mantid (Pseudomantis albofimbriata) in poor physical condition can pump up her sex pheromone production over that of her fatted rivals in order to attract male mantids not for breeding but for feeding. What perversion of natural selection is this?*

Kelsey's own mantid specimen, his personal sphinx, is posed on hind legs as if about to strike, glaring at him from her resin crypt.

"Miss Manty," he whispers, "your prayer is that a whiff of you will lure an addlepated partner to a romantic dinner for one. That's not praying, it's preying." He picks up the paperweight and locks eyes with her. "Who could resist those pleading eyes, that entomophagous grin? You are marvelous."

Dr. Barry doesn't solve the riddle to Kelsey's satisfaction. It is as if she believes the *why* is understood. Miss Manty risks death to overpower the allure of the healthy females in the area, but not to mate, rather to eat. It's a fail-safe survival mechanism. Individualism in a form rarely witnessed in the animal world outside of humans. No self-respecting species, Kelsey believes, would tolerate such sinister behavior. And yet…

"Tell me, *why*, Manty?" He speaks as if expecting a response. It's not that she *can't* talk; he believes she chooses not to. "Look me in my omnivorous eyes and tell me why it is more important for you to *mangiare* for your own good than it is for your Romeo to *scopare* for the good of your species?"

He holds the paperweight closer to his desk lamp, as if the heat will sweat the truth out of her. "If this is self-preservation, plain and simple, then why does your bug-thirsty smile say, *I live to eat* rather than the reverse? There's another lesson here, isn't there? Your victims, perhaps. Is that the key? They crawl to their deaths as if in Dracula's sway. You thrill in your thrall, don't you? Why, my monstrous, my marvelous Manty?"

He sets the mantis on his desk and swivels back to his keyboard. "There's more to you than a malnourished, man-eating minx. Stand over there and be quiet. I need to think."

# Tireet-twit-twit

*Friday, March 13*

Standing at her kitchen window with her morning coffee, June notices last night's dusting of late winter snow has her birds flocking to the feeders. "Jonesy," she says to the attentive, middle-aged Norfolk terrier sitting behind her, "if you could just scare the squirrels without scattering the birds, you could save me some money." She would like to think of the squirrels' share as a small price to pay for the year-round abundance of birds, but seed is expensive. "Maybe," she proposes, "I'll put up a better squirrel-proof feeder in the center of the yard by the vegetable garden. That'll be pretty, don't you think? We'll leave one of the other feeders where it is so you'll still have squirrels to chase."

The dog's stub of a tail wags twice at the coo in her voice.

"I knew you'd like that idea."

Her husband hated the squirrels. Doug trapped a dozen or more and relocated them to the Capitol City side of the river. "They can find their way home across land," he had said. "But they won't cross water." It makes her sad to think squirrels want so badly to get back home that it takes a river to stop them. She wonders what the yearning is for? Family? Familiar territory? The food they buried? Whatever it is, there is a way to foil them: put water between them and that for which they long. June wonders if they know what calls them is just a few hundred yards away. Is it that they don't dare swim, or does the water wash all memory away? Does fear make them forget what drew them to the water's edge, or does a God-given amnesia save them from drowning? Maybe the water speaks to them, comforts them, frees them from their yearning. She wants to believe they are all freed in the end. The mother, her mate, their kit. All freed from whatever is across the water. She wants to imagine it as a cleansing, a form of baptism. The alternative is too grim. "Lord knows," she says, her words fogging the window, "the last thing I need is to take on the sadness of squirrels."

Kelsey gazes out his office window, assessing the evidence of the pending seasonal transformation. There is little to betray spring's approach. A few imprudent crocuses have shown themselves. The rhododendron trusses are forming. Hints of buds on the magnolia and dogwoods. And all of it now dusted with a fine powdery reminder that it is still late winter.

From his study he can see the entire south side of his neighbor's house, including the weathered steps leading up to her front porch, the two lace-curtained living room windows, the second-floor bedroom window, the porthole of her master bath, and all the way back to her vegetable garden with its wire-meshed picket fence. *For a middle-aged widow living on her own,* he observes, *Mrs. Danhill does an admirable job of keeping up the house and yard, with the exception of the battered storage shed just beyond the vegetable garden.*

He window-gazes more now. He never thought about how much time he and Rose spent doing things together until they stopped. The gardening and evening walks are long over. The cooking takes less time when done without discussing his latest article, debating how much jalapeño is too much, or listening to Rose share her fresh insights into the book she is revisiting for the first time in many decades. There are gaps in the day now. He would prefer to fill them with work, but the words won't come like they used to. And if they come when he is not at his desk, they flit away before he can pin them to a page. To avoid contemplating what will be in store for a widowed, out-to-pasture professor whose latest article seems just a bit out of reach, he instead stares out his window in wonder. He knows he'd be better off doing crossword puzzles, volunteering at the Capitol City soup kitchen, and taking brisk walks rather than remaining holed up in his sarcophagus of an office. But he's troubled by what the end of his writing will signal to Rose. He knows that if she knows he is no longer working, she'll worry. He can't have her worrying about him. She's done enough of that over the course of their—god, how many years has it been? Worrying her now simply won't do. Instead he window-gazes.

He has spent weeks admiring the birds. The trees demarking the property line he shares with Mrs. Danhill form an avifauna holding area from which various sizes, colors, and temperaments negotiate their turns at her feeders. The bold ones sit in the skeletons of the dogwoods. The warier prefer the cover of the pines. He doesn't take any particular pleasure in one species or other. He watches as a bystander. He recognizes that he observes the birds with anthropomorphizing eyes. This makes observation infinitely more entertaining, if somewhat less scientific. He notes that some birds seem to act with a semblance of clannish courtesy. Juncos, sparrows, wrens, chickadees, and titmice are in this group. Others have no patience for pretense. The blue jays exhibit a brutish dominance at the feeders, which is matched only by the squirrels. The cardinals, he believes, are the most civilized of the bunch. They wait serenely above the fray, the males dressed smartly in their scarlet waistcoats, their female companions adorned in comparatively drab yellow-brown; however, in proper light, he has caught glimpses of the titillating rusty red that accessorizes the female cardinal's headdress, wings, and tail. "Ahh," he sighs, "the joy of details."

He occasionally spends the night on the small couch in his study and is awakened by the morning birdsongs. The first hint of sun is appearing earlier as spring approaches. He wishes the precipitant among the flock would delay reveille at least until dawn breaches the trees. They seem to find perches that reveal hints of light on the downward arc of the horizon. He knows there is a chronology to the songs, but he hasn't been able to attach them to their singers. Robins are first, he is reasonably sure of that much. He also knows the morning songs in the spring will be a mix of territory-marking and wooing. Other than that, and his awareness of their predation on his beloved bugs, birds are a bit of a mystery.

Some days Kelsey imagines that ornithology will be part of what's next. Other days he thinks, more realistically, that maybe he will just take up bird-watching. On these rational days, he recognizes that another "ology" is more than his dimming mind can handle. So, he pictures himself in the company of others, binoculars panning a canopy, whispering conspiratorially and trying to triangulate the source of a mysterious tireet-twit-twit. He can think of much less appealing ways to spend what will otherwise be solitary afternoons. He readily admits he's not much good at solitude.

Today, as he looks out his window, he recalls recent driveway conversations with his neighbor. They have been trivial. Mostly about their mutual desire for spring to spring. By speaking to him, Mrs. Danhill has expanded her presence in his world, a world that has been circling in on itself since he retired to care for Rose. Thinking of his neighbor is…how best to describe it? Unsettling? There must be a better word for the flutter he feels when he encounters her. Mrs. Danhill has lived next door for many years. He knows tidbits of her history. The husband's sudden death. Her son married with babies and relocated to… where was it? *She is, if memory serves, a perfectly nice woman. But what do I know?* he asks himself. *What don't I know?*

He experiences a slight adrenalin rush when he hears the desk bell's three sharp rings—*dingdingding*. He wasn't expecting them. When he last looked in on Rose less than an hour ago, she was sleeping so soundly it looked like a death rehearsal.

When he appears at her bedside, Rose says, "I hope I didn't—disturb you."

"No, it's fine. You caught me at a natural break."

"I need the bathroom."

"Happily, we have one of those."

Though walking to the bathroom is laborious, Rose considers the effort preferable to the indignity of the bedpan. As often as not, Kelsey actually welcomes the attention these trips require from him. They have so little time left.

The hospital bed groans its own form of empathic misery as he raises its head. Rose's eyes are closed and her face pinched as if even this assisted assent is uncomfortable. He helps her turn so her legs dangle off the bed.

"Careful," she pleads.

"Like the most delicate porcelain doll."

"Paper doll—more like it."

"Alexandrian papyrus perhaps?" he says, and hands her the cane.

"Don't make me laugh. I'll wet my pants." She uses the cane as a lever to propel herself off the bed.

"Sorry, but you have to admit your color has moved toward a lovely shade of Ptolemaic jaundice."

She puffs what has become her approximation of laughter. "You're not nearly—funny as you think."

"I'm saving my best material for the return trip."

She pulls her oxygen with her left hand and works the cane with the right. Kelsey walks a step behind, ready to assist as necessary, clocking the trip with his wristwatch. The walk is about fifteen feet. She is sitting on the toilet in a minute and eight seconds. Respectable but slower than last week's average. The return trip takes a minute fifteen.

As he tucks her back into bed, Kelsey says, "Gabriel called and asked if I could work in a game of squash tomorrow afternoon."

"Gabriel?" The name rouses her. "What did you say?"

"That I'd check with you, of course."

"Don't be silly. Go. It's been months."

"I didn't know how you'd feel about being alone for over two hours."

"I'll be fine. Go at nap time. I'll take a pill."

"It'll be good to see Gabriel again," Kelsey says. "And to get back on the squash court."

Speaking of Gabriel Rachlin reminds Kelsey how fond he is of his old friend and how much he has missed him. During these last two years with Rose, much of his past has irretrievably receded, lost forever to the darkness that closes in on a neglected fire. Gabriel's voice had restored a small, bright ember of that past to the present. Kelsey was uncomfortable admitting to Rose how much he was looking forward to the reunion, especially given Rose's tragic loss of Maggie Rachlin's friendship.

"It'll do you good," Rose says. "Maybe help the writing."

"I hadn't considered that. But, yes, maybe."

"Go make your date."

"Thank you." Kelsey excuses himself with a courtly bow. Rose is, after all, his *principessa*.

Rose turns to her father's photo. *I envy his call from Gabe. Two men bound by slowly disappearing women. I miss Maggie. You know about her. Her son Kyle was a therapy horse kid. When Maggie first saw Kyle smile from the saddle, his hands stretched triumphantly to the sky, she became hooked on the therapy and we became friends.*

Rose and Maggie did luncheons or went to movies together while the men played squash or hung out in the cigar parlor at Smitty's Smoke Shop. Maggie was funny and loud, with a quick laugh that rippled the surface of whatever Rose was drinking. Then Maggie lost her daughter and Rose lost Maggie. She couldn't talk to Rose about it because, Maggie said, Rose had never lost a child. How could Rose know how it felt to have a daughter raped and murdered? Colleen. Twenty-one years old. Brash and as loud as her mother. Eyes as unruly as her universally envied red curls. She had just moved into her first apartment. The washing machine in her building was being repaired. She drove to a nearby laundromat and was not seen alive again. How could Rose possibly understand the depth of the darkness into which a mother descends when she learns her daughter's body was dumped in an empty lot in Capitol City? There was nothing Rose could say. What could anyone say?

Maggie was marked by the murder. She was convinced she infected every room she entered with her toxic grief. The Rachlins moved three towns up river. Far enough that no one would recognize her, but not so far from her daughter's grave in Marrsville's Memorial Cemetery that she couldn't visit it every day. Up until a year ago, Rose would visit once or twice a month. When she became too frail, Kel would drive her over.

She would sit in the car and secretly hope to see Maggie, to hold her. Rose took poems with her—elegies and poems of grief or death mostly—and read them aloud. Sometimes, as with Johnson's *On My First Daughter*, with hope of comforting Colleen. Other times she went for herself, maybe reading Neruda's *Nothing But Death* and hoping Colleen would tell her if he'd gotten it right. Rose had struggled then, as she still does, to reconcile what she has seen of death—her mother too young; her father by choice—with what she wants to believe. The only thing she's sure of is that every death is two deaths: one intimate, ineffable, finite; the other an endless metaphor, *a barking where there are no dogs… That's right, isn't it, Colleen?*

Rose thinks losing Maggie was a sort of preparation for her own process of dying, of being alone with only Kel for company. Long before the cancer drove Rose indoors, the luncheons and movie dates had ended. She'd lost her big, loud, funny friend. She'd loved Maggie. She still would if Maggie would let her. It was mean, what Maggie had said, but a meanness racked with truth. Rose could forgive her, has forgiven her.

Rose speaks to her father but stares at a picture on the wall of a bunch of smiling kids and a horse. *She made it sound like I was missing a gene instead of a uterus. The mother gene. Apparently treating other people's children wasn't motherly enough. She couldn't believe I could ache for her, with her. That I could feel the same burning in my gut that she felt in hers. I never told her about the pregnancy. Why? A lima bean isn't the same as a daughter. I couldn't compare our losses. She wasn't trying to be mean. And maybe she was right.*

# THE MEMORIAL PARK BOYS

*Sunday, March 22*

June wonders if she is being too maternal with the boys. After thirty years of teaching elementary school, she tends to see every child as ten years old, fiercely independent but with one eye over their shoulder to make sure Mom's still in sight. The boys work hard and are reliable for the most part. And they certainly appreciate the money. But truth be told, she's less interested in the work they do than in knowing that at least for a few hours on a Saturday or Sunday afternoon they're safe from the trouble they can get into, especially down in the Memorial Park section of town. They're a bitter bunch down there. June didn't understand how bitter until the playground business.

Marrsville came together to build a fancy playground made of wood with a tower and a bridge and swings and ropes and a picket fence all around with the names of the donors and volunteers routed into the pickets by local carpenters. They built it down by the river in Colonial Park, between the soccer and baseball fields. Instead of joining in with the community construction effort, the Memorial Park folks demanded playground equipment on their side of town too. They claimed there are too many busy roads for kids to cross alone on their way to the waterfront park. And besides, they said, it's always about what the people in The Heights want. The whole of Marrsville is less than two square miles and a handful of people wouldn't stop harassing the town council until they got a swing set, slide, and monkey bars set up in an open field by the trailers across from Memorial Cemetery on the south side of the railroad tracks. *Such a tiny town,* June thinks, *and it's us versus them. They're so angry, as if people in The Heights have it in for people in Mem Park. Sometimes it feels like the Mem Park folks have it in for themselves.*

So, she worries about the boys, especially TJ. He's a good kid. She taught him in third grade. He made her laugh when he said straight out that they come up to The Heights because "you don't shovel your own snow." He comes with his little brother, Joey, who seems to depend on TJ. She never taught Joey, but she thinks he is likely a bit slow. He is small but sturdy for thirteen. He works hard and likes having a little money in his pocket. TJ has to patiently prompt him through the day. Sometimes they are joined by their cousin, Big Joe. *Big* because Joey is *Little* Joe. Big Joe's a bit of a problem. June can't say why exactly. She just doesn't particularly care for him. He is TJ's cousin and he didn't go to elementary school here. She only knows him through TJ. She has tried to be charitable and reserve judgment, but TJ has confided that Big only joins in at his mother's prompting. TJ told June his mother had said, "You're not afraid of hard work. You need to let a little of that rub off on your cousin." To which TJ had responded that he's pretty sure there isn't anything he has that Big wants rubbing off on him. That made June laugh too.

She sometimes thinks she is attached to the boys because Kevin and the grandchildren moved away. Other times she genuinely enjoys their company and doesn't give it any more thought than that. The work gets done and they laugh a lot. Big Joe keeps his distance, but he's a hard worker. In time, maybe he'll warm up to her. Maybe she'll warm up to him as well.

Kelsey has come to find his neighbor's movements almost as entertaining as the birds. He recently noticed how much of Mrs. Danhill's life plays out on the stage framed by the proscenium of his window. While his own world has become grim and increasingly insular, Mrs. Danhill long ago emerged from her mourning for her late husband and has created a lively diorama: a picture-perfect suburban playhouse replete with songbirds at the feeder, the requisite fluffy, fat cat slumbering in the bay window, and the steadfastly loyal Norfolk terrier always at her side.

He watches her comings and goings, her occasional guests'

visits over tea, her leaning over a jigsaw puzzle laid out on her coffee table. When her living room is lit just right, he can see all the way across to the umbrella stand by the front entrance and the first three steps of her staircase.

Most engaging, though, are the glimpses of her second-floor end-of-day activities. On nights when he lingers in his unlit study, he is often still awake when the light comes on in her bedroom. He's not lying in wait. This is happenstance. But he can't help watching as she passes in and out of shadow, to and from her bathroom. There's nothing prurient about it. Of course not. What he notices is the freedom of her movements. The independence that comes of having no *other* to accommodate in this most intimate of settings. She practically flits from room to room. On these nights he is treated to the silhouetted image of her sitting in her room leisurely brushing her breast-length amber hair. An exquisite detail. It calms him, this simple act; brings him back to life. Mrs. Danhill's life more than his own, but life nonetheless.

It doesn't trouble Kelsey that he finds Mrs. Danhill attractive. After all, he has not lost the capacity to appreciate the beauty of the female form. Her appeal is beyond the obvious allure of her physique, which in middle-age has retained the vigor of what he imagines was an athletic youth. She has the delicately curved length and mesomorphic legs of someone who ran or perhaps danced. He admires that she is a lady. Her bearing is very different from Rose's, even when Rose was in full bloom. Many would consider it old-fashioned, but to Kelsey Mrs. Danhill represents a bygone elegance, an appropriately prim formality that assures a woman never presents in public without her hair in place, her makeup fresh, and dressed in form-appropriate attire. When she rides her bicycle on errands, often with her gypsy dog perched in the handlebar basket, he sees the old *Life* magazine pictures of that famous actress from the fifties—the elegant one, *the calla lilies are in bloom again* one. His neighbor looks like those pictures of the actress peddling the streets of Martha's Vineyard. Mrs. Danhill brings a bit of that robust refinement to the most ordinary activity. Yes, she is a widow.

But this detail is immaterial to him. Despite the tragedy of Mr. Danhill's collapse at his son's college graduation dinner, Kelsey still sees Mrs. Danhill's current life as a welcome anodyne to his own. She has moved on and there's a lesson in that for him.

However, he's not quite sure what to make of the boys. She's recently recruited a ragtag band to perform odd jobs. The choice seems more for their benefit than hers. Not that they don't work. It's just that there seems to be as much talk and horseplay as honest labor. This isn't a snap judgment; they aren't strangers to him. They first showed up the morning after last January's blizzard. They cleared Mrs. Danhill's driveway and sidewalk, then knocked on his door. "Thanks, but no," he'd said. "I do my own shoveling." Not that he wouldn't have appreciated the help, especially since the snow was dense and wet and felt like shoveling mud. The point was he didn't want to encourage opportunistic adolescents from outside the neighborhood. Once it begins it never stops. Always another knock on the door for leaf raking or lawn mowing or window washing or whatnot. He imagined them becoming a fixture next door, an adoptive family of sorts. They didn't quite fit in the world framed by his window. Perhaps it was the asymmetry that troubled him. Three to one. His neighbor is at a disadvantage. And that places him in an awkward position. He had been content simply observing, but now he has this nagging sense of needing to balance the scales.

⁓

"Kel," Rose says, "don't you think—you're making a molehill—a mountain?"

"No, I don't," he insists. "They're like vampires. Once you invite them in and they sink their teeth into you, there's no going back. First the snow shoveling and now she has made a habit of having them around. She has them doing lawn and garden clean-up, even building raised flowerbed frames. I feel I have to keep half an eye on them. Keep them honest, as it were."

"Mrs. Danhill's a big girl. She's managed without your—guardianship so far."

"Yes, but this isn't the first time. You remember the old man."

"Harold?"

"Yes, homeless, toothless, useless Harold."

"Harold hasn't been—around for years."

"That's not the point. Harold prowled around in his hobo raincoat and cane. Given the miles he put in, I know that cane was more prop than crutch. ' 'Scuze me. The lady necstore she help me but she not home.' And he'd pull out that old pill bottle. 'I need money for my pesciption.'"

"Yes, dear, I remember—harmless, unfortunate Harold— despite your horrifying—impersonation."

"Week after week the ploy never changed," Kel persists. "Harold kept coming back as long as Mrs. Danhill kept making deals. Picking up sticks. Snipping feebly at some bushes with a set of hedge trimmers that wore him out before the bush even knew he'd been there. Old, used-up Harold. And she kept paying him."

"Kel, she was being—charitable and—he's been gone— years now."

"Yes, old Harold is gone, and now she has these boys. I feel a responsibility to keep an eye out. She is, after all, our neighbor."

"Very gallant. Now, if you're done ranting—move my tray. I'd like to rest."

"Consult the oracle," he says.

"What, dear?"

"Ask your father." Kel wags his finger at her picture. "He'll tell you I'm right."

There's a bug-eyed passion to his appeal. Rose can't figure where the anger is coming from. "Kel, stop. Take the tray."

He calms as quickly as he flared up. He picks up the tray without comment.

As he prepares to leave, she asks, "Did you turn off—the stove?"

"I believe so," he says, with not nearly the conviction she was hoping for.

"Perhaps you should—take the tray and check."

"Are you sure you're finished? You've barely touched the chili."

"A little hot," she says.

"Too hot? Just one jalapeño."

"Did you mix up your—peppers again?"

Kel tastes the chili as if for the first time. "Oh my, that is a bit incendiary."

"I'm guessing cayenne," Rose says.

"I'm sorry."

"Don't be. Not much appetite today."

"Back in a flash. Can I bring you anything else?"

"No, thank you. And Kel?"

"Yes?"

"What are you going to do—downstairs?"

"Dispose of my failed chili."

"And?"

"There is an *and*?"

"The stove."

"Ah, yes. Of course. And the stove."

"Thank you," she says, and lies back on her pillow. She lolls her head to the side and looks at the picture of her father. *Shut up.*

᪣

June is watching the boys clean out the bramble by the lilac tree when she hears a bustling behind her. The professor is tripping over the boxwood border between their yards.

"Good morning, Mrs. Danhill," he says as he regains his balance. "A beautiful day for a bit of spring cleaning."

"Good morning, Professor. Yes, it is. We're trying to get ahead of Mother Nature this year."

"In my experience she always finds a way to confound us," he says. "An April freeze is one of her favorite deceits."

"That's true," June says. "Never plant your spring pansies too soon."

"Speaking of spring gardening, I'm wondering if there is any chance I might recruit your horde of horticultural mercenaries to lay siege to the grapevine, wisteria, and moonflower gathering their respective armies on my side of the border?"

June considers her answer. Her impulse is a selfish desire not to share her crew. She has plenty for them to do on her side of the somewhat vague property line. But she checks herself and says, "I'm guessing they'd be delighted to pick up a little extra money. Why don't we ask them?" She turns to the boys. "Gentlemen, I'd like you to meet my neighbor, Professor Geddes."

The boys stop their digging and turn, offering barely audible acknowledgment.

"Good morning, gents," the professor says. "I'm wondering if I might be able to bribe you into expanding your work a bit. That area over there starts on Mrs. Danhill's property and goes to my garage. I'd like you to pull up the old vines in that section for the entire length of the garage. Interested?"

June is pretty sure the boys find his attempt at charm excessive. She certainly does. She looks to TJ, who usually handles negotiations, but Big Joe is the first to speak up.

"How much?" Big asks.

"I'm willing to pay what Mrs. Danhill pays."

"She gets a special rate. We have to charge you more."

This is the first June has heard about getting any special consideration. Big is cleverer than she has given him credit for.

"I understand," the professor says. "You do a lot of work for her." He is awkward and visibly irritated by Big's challenge. He works through his understanding out loud. "Since I don't know how much additional work I'll have in the future, I have no negotiating leverage. I suppose I'll just have to accept your premium rate. What would that be?"

"Twenty dollars an hour," Big says.

The tension of anticipation dissolves and the professor looks pleased. "Three people working for an hour should handle that section," he says. "Twenty dollars is a fair price."

"Each," Big clarifies.

"Each?" The professor's eyes widen. "So, sixty dollars?"

"Yeah. An hour."

"I see." The professor's jaw muscles betray the clenching and relaxing of his teeth. "That's a bit rich for a retired professor. Will you accept forty as a compromise?"

Big looks at TJ, who shrugs. Little Joe isn't consulted.

"Fifty," Big counters.

"What do you say to forty-five?" the professor offers. "Fifteen each for the hour. Deal?"

Big twists up one side of his mouth and kicks a clod of dirt. "I guess it depends on how much you want those vines cleared out. If it's worth fifty dollars, we have a deal."

The professor appears to be about to counter yet again when he glances over at June. She gives him the same look she would give her husband any time he tried to tip a waiter less than twenty percent. It seems to work.

"You drive a tough bargain," he concedes. "Fifty it is. Knock on the kitchen door when you're finished and we'll settle up. Good day, Mrs. Danhill."

"Bye, Professor. Watch your step."

He manages to clear the boxwoods without stumbling.

As he's leaving, it occurs to June that Professor Geddes has never asked her about any of the other help she's hired over the years. Plumbers, roofers, lawn mowing services, carpenters. But for some reason he's taken an interest in the boys. And in removing vines that have covered the unused patch of ground next to his garage the entire time they have lived there.

*I shouldn't make too much of it. I can't say I'll be unhappy to have those vines cleaned out.*

Rose has just picked up Coleridge for the first time since college and is reading *Christabel... Tis a month before the month of May, And the Spring comes slowly up this way.* Apropos. Just as she settles into the rhythm of the text, Kel appears without her having rung for him.

"Hi," she says, hoping she sounds pleasantly surprised.

"Just thought I'd peek in," he says rather absently.

She can tell he's fretting over something by the way his eyes dart about the room rather than attaching to her. "Are you okay?" Rose asks.

"Yes, fine."

"Who was that—at the back door?"

"I have the boys doing yard work for us."

"Mrs. Danhill's boys?"

"The very same."

"Is everything all right?"

"Yes…well, not entirely. No sooner had I negotiated with them for some clean up by the garage when one of them drops his shovel and comes to the kitchen door. His knock is more aggressive than necessary, as you apparently heard. I assume he's a teenager like the others, but he has facial hair and his body is more adult than nymph."

"And this troubles you?"

"No, it isn't that."

Rose senses the boy has unnerved Kel, perhaps confused him. It's not like him to rattle so easily.

Kel continues his story with the same urgency and indignation that he'd brought to his Harold recollections. "I asked him if there's a problem. 'Yeah,' the boy says, 'the vine work is harder than we thought. We need to renegotiate.' The boy speaks with such confidence, as if these are unimpeachable facts. I tell him I don't understand. The deal wasn't based on the difficulty of the work. 'Well, it is now,' he says. 'Pulling those vines is a bitch.' His word, not mine. 'We could just cut 'em instead of trying to get the roots.' No, no, I tell him, I'd like the roots out. So, I ask, How much? He says, 'The original price. Sixty dollars.'"

"Sixty dollars for—pulling weeds by the garage?" Rose says.

"Not just weeds." Kel flails his hands as if yanking them himself. "Grapevine and moonflower and ivy."

"Okay," Rose says as soothingly as she can manage. "I understand."

"We'd agreed on fifty dollars, but now the boy—I forget his name—now he wants to go back on our deal."

"I see. What did you say?"

"Well,"—Kel settles as if wanting to make sure he gets the

facts right—"I was taken aback at first, but I tried not to show it." He pulls up his shoulders and puffs his chest. "I want him to know I know his game and that I'm not intimidated. Maybe he can bully poor Mrs. Danhill, but I'm not so easy a mark. I do, however, want the work done, so I smile and say, Well, then I guess it's only fair. The boy mocks my smile and says, 'True that, Professor.'"

"True that?" Rose says.

"Yes. True that. Then he spins around and walks away before I can say anything. All I can do is watch his victorious return to his accomplices." Kel's resignation releases some of the stiffness from his spine. He sighs, sags, and continues. "All three seem to be working with a degree of purpose and élan that was lacking before the renegotiation. I suppose the few extra dollars are well spent." And with that Kel shrugs off the weight of his encounter with the boy and changes the subject. "How are you doing?"

"I'm just ducky," Rose says, trying to echo the sudden lightening of his mood. "Why did you—hire the boys? I thought you—didn't much like them."

Kel is thoughtful, deliberate with his response. "Well, Mrs. Danhill has them coming back. I've seen them work. They appear to be competent if not always efficient."

"So, Mrs. Danhill—recommended them?"

"She continues to use them. She wouldn't if she wasn't happy with their work."

"You spoke with her?"

"Yes, briefly. She introduced me to the boys."

"How is she?"

"Mrs. Danhill?"

"Yes."

"Fine, I suppose. Why?"

"No reason. I just never—hear her name and now—you've brought her up—several times recently. Seems strange. Neighbors so long—so little contact. I doubt she'd—recognize me."

"Yes, well, it hardly matters."

"Why say that?"

"It isn't as if we have a relationship with Mrs. Danhill. We aren't exactly friends. Even neighbors somehow sounds too intimate. We're people living in proximity."

"Sounds like you've—given this some thought."

He recoils slightly, as if she has suggested something untoward. She waits with heightened interest for his response.

After a moment he says, "The only thought I've given it has been in this room over the last thirty seconds. But there is something else I should be giving some serious thought to."

"Back to your bugs then?"

"Yes."

"And I to my *Christabel.*"

"Coleridge, is it? Shall I bring you a chaser of Poe?"

"Thinking of—revisiting Mrs. Shelley next. *The Last Man.* Twenty-first-century plague. To remind me—what I'll miss."

"Lovely thought," he says, just as they are interrupted by a familiar, insistent banging on the kitchen door.

"That sounds like your—new friend."

"Apparently the extortionists have finished their work. Ring if you need me."

Kel vanishes as suddenly as he appeared. *Ring if I need him. If only all of life and its foregone conclusion were so simple. Clap your hands. Rub your lamp. Click your heels. What would I wish for? Time is too easy. I've already had that. There would have to be something different about wished time. A child? Don't know that I could stand the losing or leaving. How about iron lungs like yours, Daddio? I figured I'd inherited them despite all the evidence against a shared constitution: your absence, my presence; your daring, my caution; your impetuousness, my fidelity; your fortitude, my frailty. I overestimated the significance of looking like you. Maybe that would be my wish: to be more like you. Or, better yet, that Kel were more like you. Then I could stop worrying about him and focus on feeling sorry for myself. He's going to need help. I can tell. Just like Mom, he's slowly coming apart at the seams. The stuffing's leaking out. You think we got raw deals. I'd rather go feet first than headfirst any day. You weren't there for Mom. You don't know what it's like. Kel won't know what hit him. Who was it who said I don't mind dying, I just don't want to be there when it happens? That'll be Kel. He won't be there when he goes. I'd like to wish away that horrid fate.*

*❦*

The boys work for an hour and fifteen minutes, give or take. Kelsey hadn't expected them to work overtime. He opens his wallet in front of them so they can see him remove all the cash in it. Three twenties. The tallest boy is closest to him, but he extends the money to the lead negotiator.

"There you are, gentlemen," he says. "A pleasure doing business with you."

The hirsute negotiator sucks in his cheeks as if constructing a comment about the quarter-hour unaccounted for. Then, perhaps because he is aware that Kelsey's wallet is empty, he smiles tight-lipped, snatches the three bills and says, "A pleasure doing business with you, Professor."

Kelsey accepts his acerbity as part of the deal. The negotiator hands a bill to each of the others and steps off the porch. The youngest follows. The tallest one is about to join them when Kelsey says, "You know, you'd do well to listen to your friend. He has a good head on his shoulders."

"Yes, sir," the boy says, with a curious pinch in his brow. He turns to follow his friends down the driveway.

*The tallest is polite,* Kelsey thinks. *I'll give him that. But there's something refreshing about the negotiator's directness. Refreshing in a primordial, hindbrain sort of way.*

*❦*

June watches from her front porch as the boys walk down the Geddes's driveway. She's reminded of how small they can seem, how vulnerable. Their typical smart-alecky energy is missing. They seem to be moving as if not going anywhere in particular, as if simply walking away from here. She can't help thinking about their futures. Their dreams. Do they even have dreams? Or is their future whatever they stumble into? What will that be? *They stumbled into me. There must be a reason. I'm not their teacher, but we have these moments. Moments I can use to show them kindness, a generosity of spirit. It is the least I can do.*

She calls to them from her porch. "You guys worked really hard today. Do you need anything? Water? Juice?"

"No, ma'am," TJ says. "We just finished up with the professor. We're heading back."

June takes three ten-dollar bills from her pocket and hands them to TJ.

"Here," she says. "A lot of the work you did for Professor Geddes helps me too. I appreciate it as much as he does."

Big Joe snorts. TJ glances back at the Geddes's porch.

"Thanks," TJ says.

"Same time next week?" June asks. "I'd like to build another raised bed."

TJ turns to the others, handing them each a bill. Joey smiles, manages a faint thank you, pockets his money, and shrugs. Big Joe takes his ten and rolls his eyes.

"I'll be here," TJ says.

They walk away in a loose, silent procession, Big several impatient strides ahead, Joey double-stepping to catch up, and TJ content to follow at his own unhurried pace.

Now this is a valuable detail, Kelsey notes. From his side window he has an unobstructed view of the driveway exchange that follows his settling up with the boys. Mrs. Danhill passes them additional money. He can't help thinking she is mistaking a certain charm and man-child manipulation for industriousness and initiative. He wonders, *Can she not see these boys for what they are? Is this gullibility or misplaced generosity?* Either way, he sees it as weakness, an unfortunate tick that must have developed as a result of the loss of male influence in her life. This softness makes her vulnerable. All the more reason for him to remain vigilant. *Double the watch!* he commands himself. *Once I know her better, have more details, I will offer appropriate counsel. I can help. I see things.*

# The Why

*Sunday, March 29*

1 | Sexual Deceit: A Strategem of the Weak

*Animal signals are rich in designative information. Communication theory distinguishes five subcategories of signal data: species-specific, sexual, individual, motivational and environmental information. The influence of natural selection upon the form of a signal will vary according to its informational content. For example, the variable nature of some signals and the stereotypy of others can be related to the conveyance of different types of motivational and environmental information. A single signal often conveys several different items of information, which are usually inherent in the whole signal and not represented by different parts of the signal. The form of some signals is arbitrary, but the physical structure is often directly related to information in an iconic manner, or in other ways.*

"Why do you have—all this animal signaling stuff. Cut it. Your point is—in your second paragraph.

~~Furthermore,~~ *Animal communication theory holds that in order to be evolutionarily stable, signals must on average be honest. Significant dishonesty (i.e. deception) by a subset of the population may evolve. But species survival depends on largely trustworthy intraspecies communication.*

Kel leans his head on Rose's shoulder and considers the edit. "You don't think the earlier signaling context helps?" he asks.

"It will help insomnia—if that's your intention."

Kel clutches his heart. "Ay, I'm hurt." His head slides into her lap. Rose flinches at the weight of him but lets him stay.

"And why all the fuss—about crickets? A hundred and forty species—all chirping their own chirp. Why does this matter?"

Kel props himself up on his elbow and speaks in earnest. "Tell me honestly that you're not intrigued by the fact that in North America alone crickets create over a hundred and forty distinct frequencies of chirp by rubbing their wings together, and that each species' survival depends on the male chirping the perfect frequency and the female of the species tracking him down."

"Fascinating. But your article is about—mantises not crickets. Only this paragraph matters."

—*In contrast,* *Within most mantid species for which mate-searching cues have been studied, a typical praying mantis mating system involves males searching out females guided by airborne female sex pheromones. The Femme Fatale hypothesis suggests that female mantids may be evolutionarily selected to exploit conspecific males as prey if they—the females—will benefit nutritionally from cannibalism. The physically distressed female false garden mantid exhibits this deceptive behavior.*

"This is it, right, Kel? This is what's—eating you."

"Very funny," he says, and settles back onto her lap.

Rose puts a hand under his head to assure he lands more gently this time. She tosses the pages onto the bed and rests her other hand on his chest. "Why?" she asks.

"Why what?"

"Why the deceptive—cannibalistic—mating behavior of— false garden mantid?"

"My question precisely," he says, and sits up suddenly. His earnestness reminds her of the fiery undergraduate kid she met in Colorado. He implores her to solve the riddle. "Why? It makes no sense. It's bad for the species, yet the behavior persists."

She reaches out and strokes his enviably thick gray hair. He is so alive. "Calm down, dear." Kel closes his eyes and his face relaxes. "You know that's—not what I mean. I'm asking why now? What are you looking for?" She can hear the weight in her tone. It's not intentional but she supposes it's inevitable, considering.

Kel opens his eyes. He cups her cheek in his hand and turns her face toward him. "Professor Barry's paper was just published four months ago," he explains. "Why else, my sweet?"

She turns her face into his hand and kisses it. Despite his academic ardor, his impeccable reasoning, she doesn't buy it. He is, she thinks, either incapable of understanding what he's doing or won't admit it. Both possibilities are unnerving. He doesn't normally ask her to read fragments. He waits until he has finished a draft. She suspects that he's hedging in case she gasps her last breath before he's done, that he doesn't trust his fraying brain. Or maybe he does know what he's doing and she's got it wrong. The metaphor is a bit too neat and sharply pointed for him to miss it as completely as he claims. Is it his victimhood he's probing, a weakness in himself? Or should she be taking this more personally? He knows about her father. He also knows it was her dad's idea. Why would he cast her as a villain after all these years? Kel's cruelty has never been as direct as his kindness, but it has never been unintentional either. He can be an infuriating shit when he wants to be. She just doesn't have the energy to call him on it right now.

"I'm tired," she whispers. "I think I'll nap."

*Why now?* Kelsey thinks. *What did she mean, What are you looking for? What does she know? Even in the throes of death she hears deceit, smells distance, tastes distraction, sees the slightest tremor of emotion.*

Before they were married, when Rose visited his laboratory and they looked at his specimens, he would point out the species detail to her and explain its unique place in the biosphere. But she would see the individual insect, the all but imperceptible crease in the abdomen, the twisted tarsus, the misshapen scutum, the unfamiliar pigmentation. He marveled at her powers of perception. For fifty years, he has strived to develop his skills to match hers. And every time he believes he is getting close, she sees something he has missed, perceives something he hasn't. And today she asks him, *Why now?* She knows why. He has told her. Dr. Barry is *the why.* And again, she asks, *Why now? What are you looking for?*

*I know this,* he tells himself. *I can answer with questions of my own. Important questions. Important details. I'm looking for why a species' reproductive signaling system gives advantage to…no no no no no. I'm not listening. Quiet now. Listen. I know this. I knew once. She knows this. What does she see? There are gaps. Gaps everywhere. Gaps in my knowing, in my having known. I'm missing the details. If only I could see what she sees…*

His neighbor's front door closes. Kelsey's attention is drawn to the window. She's taking her dog for his evening walk. 5:10. It is the later side of on-schedule. They hesitate at the end of the drive. The dog seems to be selecting their direction. He sniffs at a cluster of daffodils and trots off to the right. As they disappear from view, Kelsey's eyes drift to the feeders. He's treated to the sight of two goldfinches darting in and out of the upper feeder. A squirrel forages for seeds knocked to the ground by the blue jay sorting through the booty in the lower feeder. 5:15. There's a slight breeze. He raises the window another couple of inches for the revitalizing effect of the cooling air. Is that a hint of honeysuckle? Gray and white clouds drift by overhead. They seem as close as holiday parade balloons. The grays are unthreatening in this mixed-cumulus formation. If they were concentrated, the breeze and cumulative gloom would presage rain. 5:22.

The two bell chimes are calm, unhurried—*ding…ding*

"Just finishing up," he calls out. "I'll be in soon."

The clouds pass and full sun brightens the tops of the border trees. One block north a hawk rides the air for one lazy circle then glides off to the west. The traffic noise from the avenue is no louder than the evening's birds. A house sparrow ducks into a hole in the soffit. The bustle of its nest building is amplified by the gutter. 5:28. He notices his cuticles are dry and cracked. He needs to take better care of them. With all the hand washing, he should moisturize more often. He would go and get some hand cream now if he didn't think he'd miss his neighbor's return. He leans forward to see more of their route. They come into view. 5:33. Twenty-three minutes. A short walk for such a pleasant evening.

Rose, he remembers. She's probably hungry.

❧

June is disappointed that these walks around the neighborhood aren't more reassuring. A familiar child running up to pet Jonesy, a friendly exchange with the child's mother about kids and pets, the appeal of the lengthening days and the spring colors, all of this should create a renewed sense of belonging. But it doesn't anymore. She still isn't used to Kevin and the kids being out in San Francisco. She thought she would be okay with it because she has to be. But she misses them. The babies barely know her. She barely knows them. She didn't think she'd miss them this much. *Maybe,* she thinks, *I just miss the idea of them. It's so different now. Families don't stay in one place. And why should they? There's so much world out there that's not Marrsville.* She sees it at church. All the young families are new, not parish kids who grew up here and started their own families, but new families who have come here because it's cheap and convenient to the big cities. These are their starter homes. They will sell and move as soon as they need another bedroom. It's not about settling down anymore. It's about the work, something that's in short supply around here. Unless you want to work in a nail salon or a smoke shop…. *That's not fair,* she thinks. *I shouldn't say that. But there are so many of them.*

June pauses at the end of the driveway. Jonesy continues to walk until the slack runs out on his leash. He waits as June examines the front of her house. The repointed stone steps. The freshly painted railing. The wooden Welcome sign. The brass house numbers. The motionless porch swing. The silent wind chimes. The Grecian flower pot. The seasonal door wreath. It's all so familiar and suddenly strange. "What are we doing here?" she says to the dog. Jonesy looks at her as if the answer is self-evident. He strains against the leash and June follows him up the driveway.

❧

"Here you are, darling," Kelsey says, as he delivers the dinner tray to Rose. "The ribollita is your recipe with my variation: chicken and garlic added for their medicinal properties. I forgot to pick up fresh basil, so I've swapped a green salad for your preferred caprese. I hope you can forgive me."

"It's lovely, dear. Thank you."

Kelsey stacks pillows so he can sit up next to Rose on the makeshift bed.

She says, "I've caught myself drifting off—to Italy more frequently—these last few days. Not sure why."

Her voice sounds more present than usual. More vibrato, less air.

"Maybe because we had two delightful visits to Italy right about this time of year," he says, with naïve confidence in his memory.

"Close," Rose says, and grins her unintentionally ghoulish grin. "The first time—was late September. Lake Como."

"Correct. Just testing you. The second was late—"

"Early March," she says. "Tuscany and the—Ligurian Coast."

"I'm impressed. Still sharp as a thorn."

"You, however," Rose says, as playfully as she is now capable of sounding, "are more senile—by the minute. Whatever will you do—without me?"

Kelsey leans sideways, almost tipping his bed table, his nose tilted to within an inch of her ashen lips. He looks over the top of his glasses and whispers, "I will remember Italy fondly."

"What will you remember—most fondly?"

Kelsey lies back against his pillows and laces his hands behind his head. He expects memories to come flooding back, but they surface like sludge, as devoid of detail as shadowy dreams.

"Bellagio," he says, almost as a question but not quite. "We're sitting on the steps outside the restaurant drinking wine and waiting for our table. You were wrapped in your new pashmina, its hazy blue flirting with your eyes."

He is astounded when she doesn't correct him. Instead she says, "I remember the view from—the old chapel above—Ossuccio. The steep walk—rocky path—view of entire lake."

He says, "I remember making too-loud love with the shutters open and the Italian sun streaming in."

"And two bottles of wine—with lunch."

"*Vino da tavola!*" he chants.

Managing to turn her upper body toward him to under-score her question, she asks, "Kel, you don't mind—if I stick around—a little while longer, do you?"

He looks unflinchingly in her eyes. Eyes that were once a heart-stopping pale-blue with the clarity of conviction are now smoky gray. Kelsey smiles and the corners of her eyes rumple in response.

"I was just going to ask you if you would. We've had a late cancellation and the room will be available for the remainder of the season."

She snorts her amusement. "You're an idiot."

"If only you'd known before you married me."

"I did."

"Well then, you've only yourself to blame. How about breakfast on the terrace tomorrow?"

She looks out at the balcony as if calculating the effort required to walk the length of the bedroom to the café table they placed there for just such occasions.

"Sure," she says, "if I feel this good—in the morning."

He adjusts his pillows and returns to his meal.

They are both quiet for a moment. The spring's silence fills the room. The birds and neighborhood dogs are dozing.

The silence is so calming, so eerily peaceful, Rose is reluctant to break it. But it feels like the time, the appropriate mood. "Seriously," she asks, "what *will* you do—without me?"

A sudden weariness, or is it dread, rearranges Kel's face. "I thought we agreed not to speak of this."

"That was then. It's time now—don't you think?"

He sets his spoon down next to his bowl and gazes out through the French doors to some distant point in the moon-less night.

"I have asked myself this question," he says. "I would like to stay here and muddle on. But I'm no longer certain of the wisdom in that."

"Because?"

He looks as if he expects her to answer her own question. They both know the answer, but she's hoping he will finally admit it to her, say out loud what he hasn't been able to face. But he says nothing. He simply returns his gaze to the darkness. She decides they can talk about it another time.

"Will you make pancakes—for breakfast?" she asks.

His face brightens again. "Do you want pancakes?"

"I do."

"Then, *principessa,* pancakes you shall have."

"With blueberries, please."

"Done," he says.

"And sausages?"

"Of course."

They talk about nothing for nearly half an hour before the blinking of her eyes slows and he suggests they do one last bathroom break before calling it a night. Rose sighs her consent. *Eat, shit, sleep. This is a fine fucking romance.*

He cleans up the dinner dishes and considers writing before bed. He places the soup bowls on the drying rack, scans for missed items, reviews the yellow Post-its he has stuck around the kitchen one last time, and turns out the light.

Darkness swallows the room. It's the new moon. A faint reflection of a streetlamp off the dining table is the only seam in the pitch-black. He waits for his eyes to adjust before attempting to leave the kitchen. When they do, he notices a pinhole of light outside the kitchen window.

This is the view from the other side of the house. A young couple with three small children whose names he can't remember, perhaps has never known, live just beyond a row of arborvitae planted years ago by the previous owners. An impenetrable four-season hedge has formed between their houses. A child's crying, a parent's yelling, someone practicing the trombone, backyard play, an arriving or departing car, the

smell of a summer barbecue or a winter fire: this is the evidence
that they have neighbors to the south.

Kelsey stares into the wall of conjoined trees, trying to
make out the source of the tiny light. Is it eyes staring equally
blindly back at him? The light begins to dance. It blinks off
and reappears. A firefly perhaps, *Photuris lucicrescens.* No, it's too
early in the season. The light does a series of ecstatic swirls and
pirouettes, drawing exquisite arabesques that fade as quickly as
they appear. He closes his eyes, breathes and reopens them. It's
gone. No eye. No firefly. No dancing light. Just the dark matter
between two points. The gap. Event horizon. Oblivion. A great
black suburban yawn.

Back in his study the same moonless pitch envelops Mrs.
Danhill's house, though it is broken by two static lights: the
faint one over her front porch, which a large moth—*Callosamia
promethea* maybe—circles twice before disappearing into the fixture; and a bedroom desk lamp, in the soft glow of which Mrs.
Danhill brushes her hair. *No, not brushes. See the details. She strokes
slowly, lovingly, longingly.*

Eight years on and June still keeps up the ritual. But it's just
habit now. Brushing out her own hair before bed is like brushing her teeth. It's something she does while reviewing her day
and the next day's commitments. It has been years since she last
allowed herself to remember how good it felt when Doug did
it. She would sit on the edge of the bed. He would straddle her
from behind. They would talk about the day, about tomorrow,
and she would close her eyes, allowing herself to enjoy the traveling tingle of the soft bristle, wave upon wave of always tender
strokes, soothing and nurturing. It made her feel cared for, almost childlike. Now she brushes absentmindedly. Her eyes are
open. Her hands move with purpose but without any of the
care Doug brought to the task. *Why is it,* she wonders, *that we are
incapable of treating ourselves as we would have others treat us? This is the
great flaw of Luke 6:31. Of Matthew 7:12. They presume a generosity
of spirit in our treatment of ourselves. Oh no, please, don't bother, we say.*

*Don't make a fuss. I'm fine. When do we ever say, Please trouble over me? Touch me as if yours are the fingers of an angel sent to comfort me. Never. Never. Do unto others as you would have them do unto you. But heaven forbid we should treat ourselves as kindly as we treat others.*

She allows herself this moment of melancholy. Just a moment. Because, after all, there's not very much she misses about sharing her life. She misses Doug, but she can't have him back. She could fill the space he's left, but with whom? Could she find someone who would invite her to sit between his legs while he brushes her hair without any expectation that her pleasure is prelude to his? Someone who would bring her this childlike comfort without making her feel like a child? Are we allowed more than one love like that in a lifetime? Maybe her life is meant to be a celebration of the blessing that was Doug.

"Thank you," she says to the thought of her husband. "Thank you for being here. As always, please keep an eye on Kevin, Bonnie, and the kids. They're so far away. Sometimes I feel closer to you than to them. I love you. Amen."

# WISDOM IN OUR CELLS

*Easter Sunday, April 5*

This morning is another good morning. A very good morning. Rose has made her own way out to the deck. Kel helped her out of bed—using her hands this time, not by lifting from under her arms like she's a sack of bones. Once her feet were on the ground, she felt a solidity, a physical presence she thought she'd lost. Over the winter, every time she got up she'd feel the world spinning beneath her. Walking wasn't like going from here to there; it was a struggle to keep up with Earth's rotation, to avoid being flung off. But spring has been restorative.

*Maybe the sun is slowly recharging my cells,* she thinks. *Maybe there's one more anniversary left in me after all.*

Last week Rose decided the morphine was making her too sleepy all of the time. She cut back on her pills, taking one only when she was too uncomfortable to ignore the pain rather than as part of her cancer medication regimen. After her first skipped dose, she didn't feel a significant increase in discomfort, but she did feel more alert, had more energy. Her trips across the room to the deck, dragging her oxygen tank over the carpet assisted only by her cane, are having the effect of exercise, making her stronger, more aware of the power secreted within her scrawny limbs. She thinks the vitamins and juices she's had Kel add to her routine are working in ways the chemicals couldn't. Whatever the reasons, this morning she's comfortably erect in her cushioned cast-iron chair enjoying a poached egg and a fresh, warm croissant with her husband.

When she closes her eyes and runs her tongue around her lips, she can taste the nectars in the air, a reminder of what she's lost. Two years ago, her gardens were an envied feature of the annual Mary Morris Garden Club tour. Now, as she surveys them from the deck, they look more managed than cared for.

Kel can't keep up. He's not a gardener. He mows and trims, plucks and picks. But he doesn't taste the soil or speak to the buds. He'll water and deadhead, but he doesn't take the time to know the specific blooms and their idiosyncratic needs. His eye is drawn to the ladybug, not the bearded iris the bug is crawling over. The garden club offered to have a couple of members drop by now and then to help, but Rose knows how much time they put into their own gardens and club events. She didn't want them to have to babysit hers too. Last spring, she could still walk out into the yard and show Kel the black-eyed Susan she wanted him to pull out, or indicate where she wanted him to move the overgrown hosta. Now she can only point from her overlook or write up to-do lists for him. He does the big stuff, but the garden's real beauty is in its finer points, the shenanigans that have to be sensed unseen. Kel is all eyes. She secretly hopes he'll manage to leave something for the next owner to admire.

This morning's breakfast came with the latest pages of Kel's paper. He seems to be marshalling on despite her discouragement. Today it's…

## 2 | EPIGENETICS AND THE FEMME FATALE

*Dr. Barry calculated that eating just one male can enhance a starving female's body condition by about one-third and improve her fertility by nearly 40 percent. The paradox being this is at best a short-term strategy.* Entire life is short

*The female invests a tremendous amount of her life energy into signaling. The benefits are obvious and high: a substantial, easy meal. But producing any kind of signal has its costs. By focusing on pheromone production, the mantis diverts energy from egg production.* Prey! *Before she feeds on her suitor, she risks further reduction of fertility and of her general vitality. The 40 percent increase in fertility is calculated from a greatly compromised condition. She remains in a state of distress.* They're

*These facts suggest that the deceitful signaling practices of these female* bugs! *mantids are maladaptive and in the most cynical spirit of the Darwinian drive to self-preservation. It is difficult to imagine an entire species' genome selecting for the expression of a behavioral trait that leads to the diminution of the viable mating male population without allowing for the procreative process.*

*There is, however, another possibility: an epigenetic stress response not unlike those recorded in humans who experience episodes of extreme stress, such as a deadly accident, a concentration camp, childhood abuse or brutal acts of war.* What?

Rose tosses the papers on the table and leans back. "Really, Kel?" she says. "Praying mantises are—like people now?"

Kel addresses her over the top of his lowered section of the *New York Times.*

"Not like people," he corrects, "but in this case perhaps not unlike us. It's really rather brilliant if you think about it. It diminishes the role of the mantid's genotype and focuses instead on phenotype."

"But there can't possibly be—any research to support this."

"Of course there is. Read on."

*Years of study in mammals, including humans, have shown that one's personal experience and* the environmental Humans! *factors associated with it can affect which genetic traits we express. Genetic function can be changed not only by mutation, but also with an environmentally induced change to the epigenome—the layer of heritable gene regulation not tied to the DNA sequence. An epigenetic change alters phenotypic expression without changing the genotype.*

*Epigenetic expressions are controlled at the cellular and molecular level. Trauma and the extreme physical stress that accompanies it can fundamentally change the biological equilibrium within one's body. DNA damage has been shown to lead to gene silencing and other changes in the transcription of genetic messaging within cells. Our cells remember. This "wisdom" in our cells can be passed on to future generations.*

She drops the pages again. "You really expect your readers— to accept an insect's phenotype—is like a mammal's—even a human's?"

"Why not?" He leans toward her and begins gesturing as if back at the lectern. "Epigenetics would help explain the risk these females take to survive. Stress is an extremely powerful behavior modifier. An animal experiencing its own personal holocaust focuses on its immediate conditions, not on some abstract notion like the survival of the species. In its distressed state, the female mantid is focused on one thing: food. Her genes tell her that honest communication preserves the collective, but her drive to survive reprograms her microbiology."

Rose can't suppress her sigh. She hands the pages to him. He is so boyishly enthusiastic. She doesn't have the heart to tell him how misguided she thinks his entire train of thought is. Equating post-traumatic stress response in a three-inch bug that lives for six months to the *wisdom* epigenetically transferred across generations by human cells smells like bullshit to Rose. *So much time in his study is unhinging him,* she thinks. *He needs to get out more.* Insisting that he not bring in help to take care of her has been selfish. She's beginning to see the damage she's done by putting her death above his life. She knows he'll never admit he's riding into an intellectual box canyon. It's up to her to fix this.

"Kel, I'm no scientist but—you're overreaching."

Kel puts the pages back in sequence and rolls them up. He lifts the tube to his eye and looks through it at her.

"You ain't read nothin' yet," he jokes.

"Well, whatever the punchline—it's going to have to wait. I need a break."

He giggles, still staring through the rolled pages.

"What's funny?" she asks.

"You have the loveliest bouquet of calla lilies dangling from your nose. You wear them well."

"Tell me you're joking."

"Oh no. They were quite beautiful. Aubergine, I believe the color was. But they're gone now. Poof."

"You're being silly."

"No, darling. Calla lilies as clear as the nose on your face. Who was that actress—the one who says, 'The calla lilies are in bloom again...'"

"Katherine Hepburn."

"Yes! That's her. What's the rest of it?"

"'Such a strange flower, suitable to any occasion,'" Rose quotes from the movie they've watched together a dozen times.

"Yes!" he cries out. "Any occasion! So true."

She studies him. He's giddy, refusing to give up the joke. "Help me into the—recliner. I'll rest out here. What will you do?"

"Clean up and go for groceries," he says.

"Be careful."

"As you command, *mia principessa*."

"I'm serious, Kel. Be careful. You're seeing things. That's scary."

"A momentary diversion. Nothing to fear."

"You're not taking this—seriously enough. Make an appointment—with Doctor Bernstein." She stands and Kel hurries around the table to pull out her chair.

As he guides her to the recliner, he says, "Last year Geoffrey's diagnosis was mild, age-related cognitive decline with a prescription to stay mentally active. I may be another year stupider, but I'm not sick. So, what's he going to tell me to do?"

"That's a question for him—not me."

"I'll think about it. *Addio mio amante*." Kel gives her a courtly bow and goes into the bedroom. Rose is encouraged that he remembers to take grocery money from the cashbox in his nightstand. He turns and waves as he pockets the bills.

She waves back. *Christ. Hallucinating flowers in my nose. It's worse than I thought.*

✑

June hopes the service will be comforting today. With all the restlessness she's been feeling lately, one of the few things that brings her any serenity is a seat in the church she attended as a child, the church where she met Doug while playing in the handbell choir, where they married, and where their son went to nursery and Sunday school. The church bells still ring out from the brick tower that lords over the neighborhood, the one charming feature left in Marrsville. She has never worn a watch while gardening or reading on her porch swing. The bells mark the half-hours and hours between nine in the morning and six in the evening. They celebrate not only the town's earlier appeal but June's past too. Sometimes she feels her attachment to the authoritative chimes is shamefully sentimental. Then there are days like today when the bells return her to herself and she embraces them shamelessly, their perfect tones never wavering, never late, steadfast, true.

Jonesy asked to be aired just when June was going to leave the house, so she has missed most of the music that opens the service—her favorite part if she's honest—arriving just as the choir is winding up the introit. She takes a seat in the back as Pastor Butterfield leads the responsive prayer for Easter.

> One: O Christ, in your resurrection, the heavens and the earth rejoice. Alleluia! By your resurrection you broke open the gates of hell, and destroyed sin and death.
> All: Keep us victorious over sin.
> One: By your resurrection you raised the dead, and brought us from death to life.
> All: Guide us in the way of eternal life.
> One: God of mercy, we no longer look for Jesus among the dead, for he is alive and has become the Lord of life. Increase in our minds and hearts the risen life we share with Christ, and help us to grow as your people toward the fullness of eternal life with you, through Christ our Lord, who lives and reigns with you and the Holy Spirit, one God, now and forever.
> All: Amen.

June is restless and distracted without knowing why. She enjoys the hymn but finds herself glancing around at her neighbors as they lazily mouth the *Prayer of Confession*. She closes her eyes during the silent personal prayer time, but all she has to confess is that she feels no need to confess anything. No failure of character or slip of the tongue or transgression of the heart. Given the day, her lack of humility adds to her agitation. It's just a mood, she reassures herself. She can choose to ignore it. Give her thoughts over to the service, her heart over to God. But she

barely hears the readings over her own internal chatter, cannot
feel the Lord's presence given her own absence. The choir calms
her for long moments, but the noise takes over again during
the somber readings. Finally, the sermon. Pastor Butterfield is a
good man, a sincere man, though a rather tedious speaker. She's
hopeful his message will connect, put an end to this feeling of
slipping away. Her hope diminishes when he begins, as he often
does, by trying to lighten his dour message with a reference to
popular culture.

"I call today's sermon The Last Laugh. Most people have
heard the famous quip about the best way to make God laugh:
just tell Him your plans for tomorrow. In today's reading we have
the reverse situation. God tells Sarah His plans for her, and Sarah
laughs. But Sarah's laugh isn't a joyful laugh; it's a bitter, mocking,
sarcastic laugh…"

June is having trouble sitting still. She apologizes to the unfamiliar woman next to her with her two young children dressed
in their Easter best. Sarah's story is familiar and not a story June
finds particularly uplifting. A story of God's omnipotence, of
women's subservience, of Sarah's failure to trust in His word.
Why this story for Easter?

"You know the adage: fool me once, shame on you; fool me
twice, shame on me. When God repeats his promise of a child
a fourth time, Sarah reacts as most of us probably would: she
laughs in God's face. Exhausted and bitter in the wake of broken
promises, she's fed up with this test of her faith. Talk is cheap,
right? We all find ourselves in such a place in our life now and
then, when we ask ourselves what is God's plan for me?"

Pastor Butterfield's question recaptures June's attention. This
is what she has come for: a remedy for the disquiet that swells
like rolling thunder. She leans in expectantly to take in the day's
prescient message, to learn her new purpose in this old place.
But the story returns to Sarah and the message returns to Him.

"However begun, it will end in laughter. God will have the
last laugh, and everyone who hears will laugh with him."

That's it? We're all just waiting for God's punchline so we can
have a hearty group laugh when the world goes up in flames?

As the congregation rises to sing "Christ is Alive," June excuses herself, maneuvers past the kicking legs of the bored children and makes a break for the double door.

Outside the church, she takes a deep breath, settles, and decides to take the long way home. She needs the walk to clear her head of the scornful sound of God's laughter. She starts toward town. She can see the fire station is having its annual fundraiser flower sale and adds another two blocks to her route so she can pick up some hot house tulips and an Easter lily to brighten up the living room. Her house needs life.

Back home, she picks up the newspaper she stepped over on her way to church, the *Burgess County Bugle*. TJ sold her a subscription during a fundraising drive for something to do with school. She used to read it, but she doesn't much anymore. Too many stories about kids and drugs and violence. One crisis after another. It's depressing. She waves the paper at the professor, who is backing his car out of his driveway. If he notices, he gives no indication.

As soon as she enters the house, Jonesy barks at the back door. Again. A bladder infection, maybe? She places the paper and flowers on the dining table and follows him outside. She watches from the back porch as he sniffs around the grass. She inhales the nascent spring and relaxes into its Sunday, pre-lawn-mower silence.

The quiet is disturbed by a faint, unfamiliar sound. A bell, she thinks, but high-pitched, sharp. Not her church bells. This bell seems to be coming from the Geddes's house. It chimes a second time, louder. It's coming from the balcony off the second floor. June positions herself so she has a clear view over the fence. Through the neighbor's balcony railing she can just make out a slight figure sitting in a wooden recliner. She hears a third chime.

"Hello, Rose?" June calls out. She thinks she hears a response, but she can't make it out. "I'm sorry, Rose, I can't hear you. Do you need help?"

Again, there is a response, like someone with a horrible case of laryngitis.

"Rose, I'm sorry. If you'd like me to help you, ring your bell again."

*Ding ding.*

June has no idea what she's getting into by agreeing to help Rose, but for some reason it feels good and, well, normal, neighborly, useful. After all this time, Rose is reaching out to her. She is being asked to help. Divine providence, perhaps?

June puts Jonesy back inside and picks up one of her containers of tulips. Knowing Rose is on the balcony overlooking the backyard, she crosses the driveway and goes through the garden gate. The back door is unlocked. The kitchen is neat with hanging pots, blocked knives, and racked spices. Only after she's halfway across the room does she notice the Post-its. *Take Your Pills* on the cabinet. *Garbage Monday* on the trash can lid. *Lock it!* on the unlocked back door. *Turn Off Stove* on the casing of the arch leading to the dining room. As she reads each phrase, she hears it spoken in Rose's laryngitic voice.

She passes under the arch and finds a fading bouquet of what she recognizes as the local grocery store's flowers on the dining table. Several petals have fallen onto the polished black surface. A light, uniform layer of dust revealed by a slant of sunlight suggests that no one has dined at this table for a while. A glass-doored corner cabinet with its silver candlesticks, cut-glass vases, and floral china reminds her of her grandparents' house and makes the Geddeses seem older, more familiar. Leaving the dining room, she enters the foyer. Years ago, she stood here briefly speaking to Rose about something unmemorable. She does recall that the house felt dark despite the large windows; the reds and browns of the wall paint and the traditional furniture choices absorbed much of the natural light. It is that way still.

This is the first time she has been up the pictureless staircase to the second floor. She stops at the top of the stairs to get her bearings. A door to her left is open. She peeks in and recognizes it as the professor's office. The floor is littered with piles of magazines and printouts. One entire wall is a

built-in bookshelf and the remaining wall space is filled with
what appear to be small animals in glass frames. With Rose
waiting, June resists the urge to take a closer look.

Down the hallway there are two doors, one on either side.
The one on the right, toward the rear of the house, is open.
As she approaches, the smell from the open door guides
her—the smell of a root cellar or damp decaying leaves. The
door is to a bedroom and across the room are French doors
leading to a balcony. Even though she has been invited, June
can't help feeling there is something awkwardly inappropri-
ate about walking into her neighbor's bedroom. She tries not
to take too much notice of the hybrid twin bed-hospital bed
sleeping arrangement, the eclectic display of framed images
on the walls, or the odd mélange of items on the dresser. She
focuses on the French doors and the woman waiting on the
other side.

Rose is lying back in a teak recliner, a floppy-brimmed sun
hat all but covers her face. Her birdlike forearms and hands
are posed on the armrests like a sparrow prepared to take
flight but frozen by a circling hawk.

"Hello, Rose."

"Sorry to trouble you," Rose huffs from under her hat. "I
thought I might—catch Kel before he left."

June gets the sense that despite her labored speech Rose
is trying to sound as if she is perfectly capable of taking care
of herself, as if her arms are filled with groceries and she just
needs someone to open the door.

"No trouble," June says, perhaps a little too cheerily. "I've
brought you some tulips from the fire station's Easter sale."
She does her best not to betray the ache welling in her chest, a
tenderness aroused by Rose's condition. She wants to believe
it is God's ache, a sign that this woman's burden is now hers
too. June has never experienced a living person who seems to
embody the weightlessness she has been experiencing these
last few months, a physical being that does not appear to be
of this world.

"Lovely," Rose says.

"How can I help?" June asks, hoping her voice hasn't hinted at the squeamishness she feels at the prospect of touching and possibly scattering the shadow in the chair.

"Got myself down here but—can't seem to climb out." She emits a noise that approximates a laugh. "If you could help—get my feet under me."

June places the tulips on the TV table that has been positioned next to the recliner. She has to rearrange the desk bell, a water glass, and a couple of books to make room. She kneels down and sees Rose's face for the first time. If she were not in the Geddes's house, she would not recognize the hollow features as those of the woman she last saw over a year ago. She tightens her own face to hold back the sadness swelling within her and asks, in as practical and dispassionate a voice as she can, "How would you like to do this?"

They agree that June will position her forearms by the armrests and Rose will transfer her grip to them in a sort of Roman handshake. June will then gently guide Rose out of the chair. The strength remaining in the depleted woman's limbs surprises June. Though she has the appearance of a wraith, the sinew and bone still have substance. When Rose is on her feet, she tells June she can manage if June will hand her the cane. June doesn't doubt her. She steps back and Rose, cane in one hand and tank of oxygen towed by the other, makes her way across the room like a determined invalid approaching the grotto at Lourdes.

"Is there anything else I can help with while I'm here?" June asks.

"Maybe," Rose says, as she slowly blends in with the gray of the unlit bathroom.

June has no intention of being a nosy neighbor, but with nothing else to do while waiting, she takes in the room. She steps back in through the French doors and is again greeted by a fustiness that a cross breeze could cure. She is tempted to open one of the side windows, but dares not presume. The walls are painted a deep red—not as brown as oxblood or

bright as ruby, but something in between. Rose has books piled
on her bedside table. A clipboard with a crossword puzzle sits
on top of the stack. There's a partially completed jigsaw puzzle
on a card table set up in one corner. The puzzle image is of a
person sitting in a chair reading in front of a wall of books. The
nondescript spines of the books and their shelves form ninety
percent of the puzzle; it's a jigsaw challenge June would have
no interest in taking on.

There are a number of pictures on the walls. Without lighting
to separate them from the dark paint, many of the images, especially the black-and-white photographs in their black frames,
seem to be floating in rather than hanging on the walls. She has
to step closer to the offset rows of pictures to make out that they
appear to be mostly from Rose's teens, perhaps early twenties:
a tomboy in outdoor scenes with horses and tents, mountains
and rivers, rugged landscapes that aren't Pennsylvania. Some
include an older man. Her father, June guesses.

The professor—young, reed thin, handsome—appears in
some more recent color photographs with Rose. She looks at
least ten years older than in the earlier pictures. In one they
mimic American Gothic with a butterfly net instead of a pitch-
fork, and with a spectacular backdrop of primary-colored wild-
flowers that June doesn't recognize. In another, they toast the
camera from the deck of a river cruise ship traveling in a coun-
try with castles. Another has Rose holding the reins of a horse
and surrounded by a group of kids. That's the extent of their
personal photographic history. There's a colorful serigraph fea-
turing the words *Uneasy Balance* and signed Sister Mary Corita on
the opposite wall along with a photograph of a jazz quartet in
a cramped, smoky club with an illegible signature. In the space
between the French doors and the closet are reproductions of
Blake drawings hung one over the other. She recognizes the top
one as his familiar *God as an Architect* but doesn't know the piece
below it—a naked man sitting on a ledge and using a compass
to draw on a scroll. She leans in for a closer look.

"Are you a fan?"

Rose's rasp startles June. She's made it halfway across the room without June noticing.

"Of Blake? Not particularly," June says. She thinks her answer comes out sounding unintentionally dismissive, so she adds, "Though I admire some of his work, I don't always understand it. And I don't know this one."

"*Newton*," Rose says.

"Oh, I get it. You and the professor."

"Hmm, no, wouldn't say that," Rose says, with what June thinks she recognizes as a wry smile. "We're neither of us—deniers of—nor apologists for—God. But it's true there's more—Newton in the professor—than in me."

June nods despite not fully understanding what Rose wants her to glean from her comment. Rather than pursue it further, she asks, "Did you decide if there's something more I can do?"

Rose gives her a look that suggests she's choosing between a couple of responses, and then says softly but directly, "Sit with me a minute."

She leads June back out to the deck with a determined steadiness. June can't help wondering if she will exhibit such patience and resolve if she is one day forced to live at Rose's pace, to walk more slowly than time, as if the world is speeding by in the next lane over. Rose motions for June to sit opposite her at the mosaic-tiled bistro table.

"I love your table," June says, running her fingers over the uneven surface of the abstract sunflower.

"Gift from Kel's artist friend," Rose says. "She's quite talented—when sober." After a silent moment Rose puts her hands on the table as if preparing to present her side of a debate and says, "I believe you've—seen the professor recently. Correct?"

Judging by the shape it took coming out of her mouth, June experiences a queasy moment of not being certain what *seen* is supposed to mean. It occurs to her that Rose is being discreet, speaking euphemistically, as if June and the professor have struck up a friendship from which Rose has been intentionally excluded. Perhaps the professor made some comment that implies there is something about which Rose should be discreet. Rose's look hints at an impatient *Don't pretend you don't know what I'm talking about* subtext. *I'm being absurd,* June decides. *I'm reading emotion into the distortion caused by her disease.* June refuses to give the thought any more energy than it already has. She lets it go, and answers as if the only possibility is that Rose is asking if she has literally laid eyes on the professor.

"Yes, I have. We've run into one another a few times this spring."

"How does he seem to you?" Rose asks.

The direct, unambiguous question reassures June.

"Fine. Our conversations are mostly about yardwork. Why do you ask?"

"I worry about him," Rose says. "He's becoming more forgetful. Saying strange things. I'm not sure—what to make of it all."

June traces the grooves in the sunflower mosaic and considers Rose's concern. She realizes that other than what she can conclude from the Post-its, she doesn't know the professor well enough to begin to recognize his state of mind. She shrugs. "Honestly," she says, "I wouldn't know. Has he seen a doctor?"

"Last year. Nothing abnormal. But these things are new."

"Well, Rose, I can't say that I've noticed anything I would call strange."

"You will let me know—if that changes?"

The request sounds not so much as a casual agreement between friends as it does a practical appeal for cooperation between mutually interested parties. June has the sense that she is about to enter into a pact with unspecified conditions. Though she's not certain what she's agreeing to, she casually responds, "Sure." She can't help suspecting Rose assumes a level of contact between her and the professor that doesn't exist, so, in an attempt to temper Rose's expectations, she adds, "I probably won't be the first to notice, but if I do, I'll certainly let you know."

Rose accepts June's answer and drops the subject. They talk a while longer about the unusually warm weather and gardening.

June offers to slip into the Geddes's yard now and then to help care for Rose's gardens.

"That would be nice," Rose says. "Would it be too much to—walk me back to bed?"

Once she is situated, Rose sighs. "Thank you for everything."

"Oh, please," June says. "It was nothing. And don't hesitate to let me know if there's ever anything I can do."

Rose's features settle into a stiff smile and she says, with as much warmth as she can muster, "You're too kind."

&

Kelsey comes to a full stop when Mrs. Danhill walks out his back door just as he is coming through the gate with his bag of groceries. Her appearance is a delightful surprise.

"Well, hello," he manages through a broad smile. "To what do we owe the pleasure?" It takes Kelsey a dull-witted second to grasp that the circumstances of his neighbor's unplanned visit might not be good news. He drops the smile and asks, "Is everything okay?"

"Everything's fine," June says. "I heard Rose ringing her bell and since you weren't here…"

"But she's okay?" he says, and feints to Mrs. Danhill's right, prepared to dash by her should she indicate that Rose needs him.

"Yes, don't worry," she says, placing a reassuring hand on his arm. "Rose just wanted help getting up from the recliner. Everything's fine. I've put her to bed."

Mrs. Danhill's touch is warm. Redolently warm. Kelsey steps past her before turning and sighing what he hopes she perceives as merely a sigh of relief, though he knows it to be more than that. He recognizes, folded into that sigh, a puny but perceptible involuntary tingling of parasympathetic nerves, a hint, however slight, of—he's ashamed to admit—desire. The feeling is disquieting. He tries to distance himself from it.

"Thank you," he says, in as neighborly a tone as he can manage. "That was nice of you. Stay if you can. Maybe some coffee, tea?"

"Thanks, but I have to get back." She turns to leave, but before opening the gate she stops to ask, "The bell, is it a signal?"

Kelsey explains that he bought the bell when the combination of his seventy-year-old ears and Rose's vanishing voice made it difficult to hear her calling him. One ring is to let him know she is awake and would welcome, though does not require, his company. Two rings mean she could use help as soon as he is available. Three or more rings in rapid succession mean that she needs his immediate attention.

"I see," June says. "That's good to know. If you're not here, I mean." June turns away, then hesitates again. "Rose is lovely."

"Yes, she is," Kelsey says. "Thank you again."

"Happy Easter," June says.

"Yes, it is," Kelsey says, and watches Mrs. Danhill walk through his gate, marveling at how natural it looks despite it being the first time. She seems so familiar to him, as if they were friends long ago and are becoming reacquainted. It occurs to him that maybe he once knew more about her, but the details have been misplaced, lost among the fraying threads of his hippocampus like so many socks in the wash. *I don't think so. She's not someone I would forget.* As the gate closes behind her, her image remains distinct, formidable. Even her scent lingers, a faint tropical quality like coconut. He carries her touch and image and scent with him into the house. He isn't flustered by the nearness of her anymore; her presence is that of a neighbor, a friend. How fortunate for Rose to have had time with her today.

✍

Kel all but bounds into the room grinning like the canary-eating cat.

"*Ciao, passerotta. Come va!*"

"My, aren't we chipper," Rose says.

"It's a very nice day, is it not?"

"Yes, it is."

"And unseasonably warm," Kel says. "I find it enlivening. And you?"

"I don't disagree."

"So, we're both chipper."

"Did you see Mrs. Danhill—on your way in?"

"Just for a moment."

"And that's what got you—chirping?" she suggests.

"Well, not so much the messenger as the message," Kel says. "She told me you two had a lovely visit."

"We did. I wonder, does Mrs. Danhill—have the same cheering effect—on you as on me?"

"I can't say as I've thought much about it. Our conversations are not the cheering sort. More perfunctory and transactional. Why do you ask?"

"I enjoyed our visit. I'd like her to come back. Soon, if possible."

"I can certainly ask her if you'd like. Do you have a day in mind?"

"Are you meeting Gabe again soon?"

"We're hoping to get a game in on Wednesday. Or is it Friday. I've forgotten. I'll have to call him."

"You seem to be—making a habit of forgetting. Write it down. When you know, please ask Mrs. Danhill if—she can visit while you're out."

"Certainly, my *Papilio socialis*. It's nice to see you emerge from your cocoon."

"It's spring after all," Rose says.

"It is indeed."

# A Visitation

Kelsey is napping on the couch in his office when the sharp hiss of tearing fabric wakes him. He cannot place the sound. He sits up and waits for it to happen again and…there…it's outside. He approaches the window anticipating that he'll discover work going on next door involving the use of weed-blocking cloth or the rending of old T-shirts into rags. But there's no one in the backyard. No Mrs. Danhill. No Mem Park boys. The disembodied rasp is coming from off to his left. He follows it and discovers a pair of turkey vultures sitting atop his neighbor's vine-covered storage shed, empty despite the suggestion made by the padlock on the sagging double doors with their broken window panes that there is something inside to protect. There's a hole in the roof that was created by a falling branch two years ago. The birds are perfectly cast as macabre ornamentation to the dilapidated building.

Kelsey finds the sight of them not nearly as disturbing as their sound. These dark sentinels, though homely, are cousins of the sacred, golden-hued, bearded transporters of Tibetan souls. He's relieved to see that the hoarse whisper that lured him from his chair emanates from birds—funereal, prehistoric, unsettling with their blood-red heads—but birds, no less and no more. Kelsey admires their timelessness. He is convinced they are an evolutionary end state, long ago having achieved the optimum form for their carrion-cleansing function. No bird-watcher is likely to tell the story of taking up the hobby after marveling at their wobbly orbit and inelegant seven-fingered wings. Yet experiencing how their presence dominates the view out his window, Kelsey cannot help feeling awe and seeing splendor that is made greater by its symbolism: patience, renewal, devourers of death.

"Welcome, friends," he says to his window. "What an auspicious visitation. I hope you find the accommodations to your liking. It is a quiet neighborhood when the boys aren't mucking about. And I'm sure Mrs. Danhill will negotiate favorable terms for the use of her shed. You'll find she's a respectable and respectful landlord."

A single ding sounds down the hall. "Excuse me," Kelsey says. "Duty calls."

Rose is sitting up in bed with a book in her lap when he walks in.

"*Hai suonato?*" he says.

"Sorry to interrupt. I didn't mean to—pull you away. Just curious who you're—talking to?"

"Prospective tenants next door," he says. "A couple of turkey vultures are considering Mrs. Danhill's shed as a roost."

"You're talking to vultures?"

"Yes. Stunning. So incongruous. And the sound they make. Underworldly."

"You're talking to them?"

"If we are congenial, perhaps they'll move in. They would be a remarkable addition to the neighborhood. Would you like to introduce yourself? You could see them from the balcony if you'd like to vulture out."

"I'm afraid they'd mistake me—for carrion."

"Well, there's that to consider. You do have your cane though, to fend them off."

"I'll pass. Share my regrets."

"Anything else while I'm here?"

"Yes," she says, and pats her covers until she locates her bookmark. She sets the book on the nightstand, tosses off her covers, and begins to maneuver herself out of bed. Kelsey hurries around to intercept her in case she gets too ambitious. "Set me up—at the jigsaw puzzle," she says.

They make their way to the card table across the room

on which is laid out a particularly inscrutable thousand-piece Ravensburger puzzle that Rose is nibbling away at. Kelsey can't imagine the attraction, but then he doesn't share her infatuation with puzzles, either pictorial or the crosswords. The image she's currently piecing together features one floor-to-ceiling wall of a glorious personal library. It is an illustration, so the spines of the hundreds of books are nondescript and have no titles. In the lower left corner, the library's anonymous owner is reading, his or her body obscured by one wing of a wingback chair, legs extended, ankles crossed. Rose has completed the outer edges and now focuses what little attention she invests in the puzzle on that lower left section where the chair, reader, and two cats provide helpful visual clues. Kelsey suspects Rose chose this puzzle as a tweak of Death's skinless nose; if He allows her to finish, He'll have to hover about for quite some time.

"Looks like you've assembled more books on your bedside table than you have put together in this puzzle," he teases.

"Who asked you?"

Kelsey watches her examine several pieces with her magnifying glass and select the one that completes a cat's tail. She victoriously taps it into place, sticks out her tongue, and directs a raspberry in his general direction. "So there. Go back to your vultures."

*There she is.* Kelsey grins to himself. The bravado, though puny in comparison to those distant days, brings to mind his old lover. The woman who tried to teach him to ride horses in the valleys and foothills of Boulder. Her mounts would cheerfully serve her, bending their powerful bodies to her will at the slightest flick of her wrist or nudge of her thigh. She rode. He was carried. The animals tolerated him, responding more to the movement of Rose's lead horse than to any guidance Kelsey tried to provide. And he deferred to them, asserting himself only when Rose directed him to shorten or slack his reins, or to prod his mount with a heel to its belly. "You have to let them know who's boss," she had coached him, but no amount of clucking or kicking or tugging could fool the horses into granting him any dominion. He settled for their agreement not to attempt to dislodge him from the saddle. Kelsey allows this perfect memory to transport him back to his office.

The vultures have left, if they were ever there. Rose is right about the forgetting, of course. And he hasn't even mentioned the Post-its or getting lost on his way to his last squash game with Gabriel. If he hadn't needed gas, how far would he have driven before realizing his mistake? "It happens to everyone," Gabriel had said. "Don't worry about it until you start finding your squash balls in the vegetable drawer." "First time for me," Kelsey had told him, but that was a lie. He had chalked up the previous times to being distracted by a story on the radio, or letting his mind drift to his latest article. That, he told him-self, could happen to anyone. But the truth is he can tell the difference. He knows being distracted isn't the same as being blind. It comes down to the systematic collusion of holes. Like tiny terrorist cells, the holes band together and cast their wicked shadow where before there were no holes. They eclipse the perfect certainty that still fills most of the vast darkness between neurons. They dull still-vigorous axons that bridge the light-years between thoughts and actions. He is aware of the shadows. He senses their presence always. Living life between them is treacherous. A life of little lies. Lies mostly, he's begin-ning to realize, to himself.

# The Significance of Smallness

*Friday, April 10*

Rose is sitting at the sunflower table looking unexpectedly regal. She's wearing a colorful sundress and her signature floppy-brimmed hat. The combination of June knowing what to expect and Rose having planned for the visit eliminates the dire feeling of their first meeting. The professor has prepared a small platter of fruit and nuts and a pot of tea.

"Thank you for coming," Rose says.

"Of course," June says. "I was so happy when the professor asked." It's a white lie. June wasn't sure why Rose would want to see her other than to get another report on the professor. She feels a bit like a spy with nothing to report. "Are you comfortable sitting? Would you prefer the recliner?"

"This is fine for now. Would you pour me—a cup of that tea?"

"Of course. Some fruit too?"

"Sure."

The week has been good to Rose. There is color in her cheeks. Her breathing is more relaxed. Her speech not quite so halting. June is sure part of the reason Rose seems more vital this time is because she expected to see less life in Rose than she had seen on Sunday.

"You look much better today," June says. "How are you feeling?"

"Thank you. I feel better. The sun and mild weather. Less morphine. A bit of the fog—has lifted."

"That's great," June says.

There is a brief, awkward silence, so June follows up with, "Is there something in particular you want to talk to me about?"

"Not really. I'm just—curious about you. You and Kel seem to be—getting along. I don't want to miss out."

And just like that June is swept back to where they left off in their last conversation. It bothers her, this notion that she and the professor have established a rapport that extends beyond a few casual exchanges about lawn work.

"Well," June says, "the professor and I have talked about clearing vines and branches, and the nice spring weather. So, you haven't missed out on much. Frankly, our conversation, yours and mine, was much more interesting."

"I can only speak from—what I see. And Kel seems in— such good spirits—after you two have been chatting."

"He does? That's nice." Rose doesn't respond, so June takes the opportunity to change the subject. "I'm curious about the picture of you with the horse and children."

Rose sips her tea as if taking a moment to adjust to the shift in topic. "That was taken—during one of my—group equine therapy sessions."

"Equine therapy? For the horses or the kids?"

"The kids mainly. But it was—good for the horses too."

"What is the therapy for?"

"Autism. Trauma. Low self-esteem," Rose says.

"I've never heard of equine therapy. How did you learn about it?"

"I put my two favorite things—together. Horses and child psychology."

"That's wonderful," June says. "The kids in the picture look so excited, so happy. It's hard to imagine them being troubled."

"It's hard not to smile—around horses."

"How does the therapy work?"

Rose cradles her tea and stares into it as if reading its leaves. "Horses know us better—than we know ourselves. You have to find horses—that want to use their—powers for good."

"So, the riding is the therapy?"

"The riding. Brushing. Feeding. Hugging. Shit shoveling."

"It sounds wonderful," June says. "Except for that last part."

"Excuse my French."

"No need. I've dealt with my share of kids and shit."

They both laugh. Rose's devolves into a slight cough. June gives her a moment to catch her breath.

"Are any of the kids in the picture yours?" she asks.

Rose smiles the embodiment of a wan smile. "All of them."

"No, I mean—"

"I know what you mean," Rose interrupts.

"I'm sorry. I didn't mean to…"

"It's fine. I could never—have my own."

"Rose, you don't need to…honestly. I'm sorry I brought it up."

"Horseback riding accident—of all things. My first brush with death."

"Oh, my goodness. That's awful."

"Long time ago," Rose says.

"Still. It must be hard to talk about."

"Not anymore."

"Well, it's a shame. You would've been a wonderful mother."

Rose grins. "I'm not so sure. Raising Kel has been—challenge enough for me."

"I don't believe that for a minute. He's a perfect gentleman."

"Then I've done well."

June laughs. "Yes, you have. Where did you two meet?"

"In biology class—at the U of—Colorado. He fell in love with bugs." Rose pauses, rolls her teacup between her palms and continues. "This is where I should say—I fell in love with him."

"But?" June prompts.

"But I didn't. Not at first. He was smart. Funny. Handsome in a soft—East Coast sort of way. He amused me. Asked me to do—interesting things. Other boys would say—go to a movie, party, game. Kel would ask—to go butterfly hunting."

"How romantic," June says.

"We both loved the outdoors—but differently. My eyes were always up. He was always—looking down. Taking in square inch—at a time. Like a child. Hypnotized by—ants working over—grub carcass. Or a single bee on—particular flower. Deer could be grazing—a few yards away. He'd be—focused on that bee till—it flew off. He'd look up and—be startled by—the sudden grandeur of the world."

June nods and smiles as she pictures the scene. "So, I take it you took him up on his unconventional dates."

"Yes, though they weren't—really dates. He knew I was local. Used me as—tour guide. He would describe a setting—ask me if I knew—a place like it. He had come west from—not far from here."

"What was he doing in Colorado?"

"Getting away. An orphan. Only child. Parents killed in a car accident—senior year high school. Picked Colorado—throwing a dart. Dabbled in philosophy—until he took biology."

"That's quite a story and a big leap from philosophy to insects."

Rose nods and sips her tea. June gives her time to catch her breath.

"He's attracted to—the significance of smallness. How much depends on—tiniest creatures."

"It's true, isn't it?" June says. "My gardens remind me of it, humble me, all the time."

Rose closes her eyes for a moment. June thinks she may have worn her out. But her eyes open again and Rose smiles as if to indicate she is enjoying talking about her college days.

"And you?" June asks. "Did you always want to be a psychologist?"

"I was going to teach. But the damaged kids were—more interesting."

"So, you switched from education to psychology?"

Rose nods and takes another sip.

"When did you stop working with kids?"

"Six, seven years ago."

"Because of your illness?"

"Couldn't keep up anymore."

"Did you know you were sick?"

"Eh," Rose says, dismissively. "Knew and not. Denied it—long as I could."

"You didn't know it was cancer?"

"Knew something wasn't right."

"What did your doctor tell you?"

"Quit smoking." Rose sets her teacup down. "And now you're—all caught up on me. Let's talk about you."

*Caught up?* June thinks. *We've barely begun.* She has so many more questions for Rose. About how she finally fell in love. About all the years between butterfly collecting and the lung cancer. About being childless and surrounded by children. But there's time, she decides. Not a lot, but enough, she hopes. Each unanswered question is a reason to come back, to comfort Rose, to stay in Marrsville.

⋖⋗

Between serves Kelsey says, "Our neighbor is visiting Rose today."

As a rule, he and Gabriel don't talk about their wives anymore. The subject of wives hasn't been a pleasant topic since Gabriel's daughter was murdered. They kept their squash dates through the ordeal so Gabriel could hit something as hard as humanly possible. For over a year, until after the trial, they didn't even keep score. When Maggie and Rose sank deeper into their respective miseries, the men agreed to keep their talk small and wife-free. Yet, for some reason, today Kelsey just blurts it out.

Gabriel stops the ball with the side of his foot and flicks it onto the face of his racquet. He balances the ball, thinks for a moment, and says, "And that is remarkable because…?"

It's an excellent question, Kelsey realizes. Of course Gabriel would assume Rose would have visitors now and again. He probably assumes Kelsey arranges for someone to be there in his absence. That *someone* might turn out to be his neighbor would be manifestly unremarkable.

"Because," Kelsey says, "this is the first time in all the years she has lived next door that Rose has invited her over."

"It's a good thing then," Gabriel suggests.

Kelsey has to think about his answer. He tries to imagine what *good* would look like in this situation. "I hope so," he says.

"Why would it not be? Do you think she's after your silverware?"

Kelsey grants him half a smile. "Hmm, I didn't think of that."

"What have you thought of?"

As the words assembling themselves worm their way toward his tongue, Kelsey experiences a nanosecond of awareness that perhaps he should halt their progress, that he doesn't fully appreciate their meaning, doesn't really know what it is he is trying to say and yet he says, "She was my friend first."

The ball rolls off Gabriel's racquet onto the court. He watches it until it stops, then says, "By *friend* you mean...?"

"Oh dear, that does sound a bit ambiguous. No, nothing so interesting as that. Just that after years of barely noticing Mrs. Danhill, this spring we have become acquainted. Conversationally, that is. Quite innocent."

Gabriel retrieves the ball and takes it in hand this time. "And Mr. Danhill?" he asks.

"Dead," Kelsey says. "Many years now."

Gabriel pinches his eyes closed for a second, opens them. "I remember this. At a party, right?"

"His son's graduation," Kelsey says.

"That's right. Were you at the party?"

"No, we weren't friends then. We attended the service with the rest of the neighborhood."

"And so," Gabriel says, "we've looped back to this visit being remarkable why?"

"It's been a while since Rose has had a confidante," Kelsey says. "Not since, well, Maggie. It's been that long since I've been in a position of wondering what she might be sharing with someone else."

Gabriel takes his position at the service line. "I can't decide if you sound like you have something to hide, or if you're jealous, or if your jealousy is what you're trying to hide. Whatever the case, I don't think I want to know. Nine serving seven. Ready?"

"What have you done?" Kelsey says, scolding himself for trying to navigate a detoured route home while at the same time
contemplating jealousy as a factor in reproductive paradigms.
"Focus. Remember. One thing at a time."

Gabriel planted the seed with their on-court conversation,
then on the way home it hit him: mantid jealousy. If I can't
have it, neither can you. He sees it now. It fits. "Oh, you sly Ms.
Manty," he says to the windshield. "I knew there was more to
it."

*Stop now. You need to get your bearings. Concentrate. The shopping
mall is on the right. Do I remember now? Pay attention to details. Lose the
details and you lose your way.*

Home is obscured by an internal fog. "See the tree," he in-
structs himself, "not the woods. Ah, the large oak, yes. Straight
on here. And there's the nursery. Right at the light. That's it."
He remembers now.

⌀

Kel wanders into the bedroom and takes no notice of Rose
sitting at the café table. She finds his lack of attention odd. She
watches him as he sorts through his gym bag and begins to un-
dress. He seems lost in the menial task of preparing to shower.

"Gone longer than usual," she says. "Did you have—a good
game?"

He continues to the bathroom as if he doesn't hear her. He
turns on the shower and returns to the bedroom.

"Kel, are you okay?"

He hesitates in the middle of the bedroom. He looks surprised to see her. "Rose, there you are. Sorry, darling. What was
that?"

"Can't you hear me?"

"Just a bit distracted. The article, you know. Ideas. What do
you need?"

"Nothing. I was just saying—you were gone—longer than
usual."

"Yes, well, we did sort of loose track of time. Sorry."

"No need to apologize. June and I had—another lovely visit. You just missed her."

He looks at her quizzically. "June?"

At first, she thinks he's kidding. But his expression, serious and searching, says he's not.

"Our neighbor. Mrs. Danhill," Rose says.

"Oh yes, of course. June, is it?"

"Surely you remember her—first name?"

Kel pulls off his socks and tosses them in the laundry basket. "Don't know that I ever knew it. But you know me with names. Hopeless."

"So, she's Mrs. Danhill to you—because you can't remember—her first name?"

He removes his shorts and stands naked before her. "Not to worry. I don't consider us to be on a first name basis anyway."

"Well, how could you be—if you don't know it?"

"I'm sorry, dear, why are we discussing this?" He is audibly shaken, the occasional tremors she sees in his hands this time affecting his voice. "If I choose to keep a certain respectful formality between Mrs. Danhill and myself, I don't think that's grounds for a federal inquiry into the limitations of my episodic memory."

"Calm down, dear. Just a bad joke. Take your shower before—the hot water is gone."

He sulks his way to the bathroom. Rose makes her own way back in from the deck.

# Speak of the Devil

*Wednesday, April 22*

June carries a tea tray upstairs. She has brought homemade cookies, chocolate dipped, Rose's favorite. June is enjoying these more regular, shorter visits. When Rose first asked if she would come by more often, June had surprised herself by hesitating.

"Are you not feeling well?" she had asked. When Rose assured June that she was feeling much better than she had a right to and was convinced the visits were part of the reason, June was unable to take the answer at face value. She suspected there was more to it. "Rose," she'd asked, "is this about the professor?" The faint glow Rose had conjured a moment before the question was asked faded as she considered her response. June immediately sensed there was a tougher ask folded into Rose's request, something that would come across less as a deepening of their friendship and more like caretaking. After her moment of reflection, Rose had admitted, "I'm worried about him."

They had spent much of that visit discussing what Rose had noticed over the last few months: the repetition, the uncharacteristic outbursts of frustration, the occasional tremors, the slow progress on, and strangeness of, the professor's latest scientific article. June had asked if they had gotten a formal diagnosis. Rose said the doctor had chalked up the symptoms to aging. If his decline had another name, no one had spoken it yet.

"They should do some tests," June had suggested. "It might be something treatable. A low-grade infection or inflammation. You never know." To which Rose had closed her eyes and sighed impatiently. "He hasn't fallen or—suffered any injuries," she'd said. "The lucky bastard—hasn't had so much as—a cold since—I don't remember when."

For the first time, June had seen the fear. She knew that her being around more would not so much be to keep an eye on the professor as it would be to reassure Rose. "Sure," June had said. "I'd be happy to come by more often. But we'd better warn the professor," she had joked. "Wouldn't want him thinking we're plotting anything."

"Yes," Rose had agreed. "I'll tell him. I'm sure he'll be—fine with it."

And Rose was right.

Today June's visit again coincides with Kelsey's squash game. She brought the cookies but made the tea in the Geddes's kitchen. She is using the visits as opportunities to get an idea of how the professor is doing with his housekeeping and with Rose's care. Depending on when she arrives, the kitchen usually gives away the latest meal he has prepared. June has noticed how simple the menus have become. For breakfast he will fix fresh fruit, yogurt, oatmeal, the occasional scrambled egg with sausage or bacon. Canned soups are frequent lunches. He still grills a cheese sandwich now and then, maybe cooks up hot dogs and beans. She's seen remnants of tuna salad served on a bed of lettuce as well. The freezer is well-stocked with things that make dinner manageable—meat patties, burritos, french fries, small pizzas, frozen vegetables. He keeps a grocery list on the refrigerator door. He's quite organized. Even the Post-its seem not so much the crutches of a hobbled brain as a testament to his ingenuity, a choice not to allow himself to be troubled by the trivial. She had asked the professor if he would mind if she dropped off leftovers now and then.

"As I'm sure you can appreciate, cooking for one is difficult," she'd said. "I often have an extra serving or two, if you're interested."

He had welcomed the gesture and now had a couple of June's dinners—a vegetable lasagna and a meatloaf—wrapped and labelled in their freezer. She is gladdened by how easily he has taken to her becoming a more frequent presence in their lives. She had thought it might disrupt his routine or feel like an intrusion. But he has been fine with it, even warm.

Now, making her way through the Geddes's bedroom, June is reminded of something else she has been meaning to ask. She places the tray on the sunflower table and hands a teacup and two cookies to Rose.

"Thank you," Rose says. Somehow delight registers on her withered features.

June begins the day's conversation with, "Tell me about the photograph on your nightstand."

Rose sips her tea and looks across the room as if to confirm which picture June is referring to, though there's only one. "That was," Rose says slowly, "the incorrigible rover—I called Dad."

June laughs. "That sounds like a generously euphemistic description. You must have been close. He's on your wall too."

"Close?" Rose chuckles. "Mostly I chased after him. Whenever I got too close—he'd take a step or two away. But he never left me. Credit where due."

"Is he still alive?"

"No," Rose says, and presses her lips together to hold in whatever might have followed.

"How long ago?"

"Ten years. A stroke."

"I'm sorry. I hope it was quick. That's the only consolation I take from Doug's death. He never knew what hit him. No suffering. No tubes."

One corner of Rose's mouth lifts and she says, "Oh, he knew what hit him. But, yes, it was quick."

June's not sure exactly what to make of Rose's reply, but she leaves it alone and asks instead, "No pictures of your mom?"

The answer to this question seems to be in the trees across the backyard. "Mom and I didn't—see eye to eye. Particularly about Dad."

"Oh, that's a shame," June says. "I'm sorry to bring all this up. I had no idea—"

"Don't be. I'm a big girl now. Water under the bridge."

"Rose Geddes, you love to play the tough old bird, but I don't think you're quite as tough as you want me to believe."

June eases back in her chair and hugs her tea close to her chest. "There's a soft spot in your heart that you fear people will discover. Like you think of it as your Achilles heel."

Rose coughs a laugh. "Do I look like—someone whose only—weakness is—a soft right ventricle?"

They exchange sad smiles. "Still," June persists, "I can see it. You asked me over, didn't you? We both know that wasn't just for my company and cookies."

Rose's opaque eyes stare thoughtfully at June. There is a long silence that neither of them is uncomfortable with followed by a knock at the front door.

"Are you expecting anyone?" June asks.

Rose shakes her head.

June reaches the door just as the visitor strikes again, this time using the lion's-head door knocker. She opens the door to a copper-skinned man nearly as tall as the door. June's appearance confuses him and he steps back.

"Hi," he says awkwardly. He has close-cropped hair, gray at the temples. He's dressed in gym clothes. The color of his lean legs provides a healthy contrast to his white shorts, white calf-height socks, and white sneakers. "I'm sorry. I'm looking for the Geddes."

"You have the right house. I'm June, the neighbor on that side. Just visiting."

"Nice to meet you, June. I'm Gabriel. Kelsey's friend."

June tenses in preparation for unpleasant news. "It's nice to meet you, too, but aren't you supposed to be playing squash with the professor right now?"

"I thought so. But he didn't show up. I waited until they made me give up the court. I tried calling his cell but there's no answer."

"That's not good," June says. "Please, come in."

"He's not here either?" Gabriel asks.

"He left about forty-five minutes ago."

"Let me try his cell again," Gabriel says. "I haven't been able to get an answer yet, but it's not unusual for Kel to ignore calls." Gabriel taps the surface of his phone and a moment later they both hear a persistent, muted sound of crickets coming from the living room. On the floor by the writing desk is the professor's chirping gym bag. "Okay," Gabriel says. "I better go look for him."

"Has he ever done this before?" June asks.

"Not to me. He generally shows up a little late, but never not at all."

"Maybe Rose would know where he might have gone," June suggests.

"I'd hate to trouble Rose with this until we know more. How is she?"

"She's doing well, considering. Would you like to say hi?"

Gabriel slides his hands into the pockets of his warm-up jacket. He looks at the staircase as if it represents a physical challenge he's not up to. "I don't think that's a great idea," he says. "What with Kelsey missing, I really should try to track him down."

"Maybe she'll have some idea where—" June cuts herself off when she recognizes the sound of tires on the gravel driveway. They both turn and watch through the living room windows as Kelsey pulls in. "Speak of the devil," says June.

Gabriel and June go to the kitchen so they can meet Kelsey at the back door. They both watch without comment as Kelsey gets out of the car and walks to the trunk. He lifts out two grocery bags, uses his elbow to lower the trunk, and walks whistling to the house.

When he reaches the porch, June opens the door and Gabriel steps out to greet him.

"Gabriel!" the professor says, with what strikes June as exaggerated exuberance. "What a great surprise."

"You weren't answering your phone," Gabriel says. "I was worried."

"Worried?" Kelsey hugs his grocery bags tighter. "What about?"

"You didn't show up for our game."

"That was today? I'm sure we said Wednesday."

"Yes," Gabriel says. "Wednesday at three."

"That's it," Kelsey says. "I even have it written on the calendar."

"Today is Wednesday, Professor," June interjects.

Kelsey looks at her as if he thinks she is testing him, then appears to realize he has already failed the test. He closes his eyes for a breath, opens them, and says, "Stupid. I'm so sorry I worried you, Gabriel. I've got my days twisted. This is the thing about these unscheduled lives we lead. No routines to help us keep the days straight. They run together sometimes."

"I know what you mean," Gabriel says, with forced reassurance. He places a hand on Kelsey's shoulder. "I'm glad you're okay."

"We'll reschedule," the professor says, and starts shuffling about looking for a place to set his grocery bags. "Let's do it now while we're thinking about it."

Gabriel raises his hand to settle the professor, who takes the cue and rocks back on his heels. "No rush," Gabriel says. "Put your groceries away. Catch your breath. When you have a minute, check your calendar and let me know what works for you. I've got to head home."

"Yes. Okay. Will do. I'm sorry."

"No worries," Gabriel says. "Give Rose my best. Nice meeting you, June. I'll let myself out."

"Thank you," June says as Gabriel passes her on the way back to the front door. Gabriel raises his eyebrows but says nothing. June turns her attention to the professor. "Here," she says, "let me take that." He surrenders one of the grocery bags and she places it on the counter. A quick visual inventory reveals most of the contents to be duplicates of items already in the refrigerator or pantry.

"I'll put this stuff away," the professor says. "You should be with Rose."

"You sure?" June says. She hopes her question doesn't carry any suggestion that she believes he is incapable of putting the groceries away. "I'm happy to help," she adds.

"Quite sure," he says. "Happy wife, happy life."

The cliché doesn't sound like something the professor

would normally say without putting his own peculiar twist to it. June reads it as a nervous echoing of her own use of the word happy. "Okay," she says, trying to convince herself that he is. "Come up and join us when you're done."

June's leaving the room releases the tension that has Kelsey gripping the remaining grocery bag like a life preserver. He sets the bag on the counter, shakes out his arm, shrugs and releases his shoulders. Had it shown, he wonders, how tightly he was holding himself, how desperately he was trying to keep the loose ends from unraveling? Gabriel's appearance reminded him that he'd set out for the gym. He remembers reaching the intersection with the supermarket on his left. The light was red. He'd sat there for a moment and his attention drifted. He can't recall what distracted him. Something on the radio. Someone familiar walking up the street. Whatever it was, when the person behind him impatiently honked, the jolt pushed his original intention aside, and out of habit he turned into the store parking lot. His new mission became a grocery shopping trip. He assembles these bits of memory as he puts the groceries away and reconstructs the events like a technician rebooting a crashed computer.

The last several days have been so ordinary, so reassuringly uneventful that Kelsey struggles with this crossing of wires. Mrs. Danhill's more frequent visits have brought the house back to life. The food she shares has lessened his burden and added welcome variation to their weekly menu. Rose's eyes have brightened despite, or perhaps in spite of, the persistent reminders of how compromised she is. Remarkably, she only uses her morphine's full potency when she needs help sleeping. Most days she is able to tolerate the pain and actually uses it as a barometer of her inexorable progression toward the day she will no longer feel any pain. It would not be an exaggeration to say that Mrs. Danhill has, in a small but significant way, returned Rose to him and brought renewed normalcy to their life. And now this. It has to stop. He has no choice but to put an end to these careless lapses in concentration. He's making himself a distraction. It isn't fair. Not fair to Rose or Mrs. Danhill.

*Pull yourself together. There's work to do. Much life to be lived.*

≈

"I don't understand," Rose says. "He was clear about—his squash date. We spoke at lunch."

"Are you sure he was talking about today?" June asks.

"Of course. It was arranged—around your visit."

"Rose, is this happening a lot?"

Rose mulls her response. She doesn't want to lie, but neither does she relish the prospect of resurrecting talk of taking Kel to the doctor. Giving his condition a name, she is convinced, will only complicate what little life together they have left. "Not that I know of," she says. "He has always been—a bit distracted. But this is new."

"Well, you know how I feel about it," June says. "If you want, I can take him. I'll even talk to the doctor about the results. I don't mind."

"Let's not fret over it—too much. He didn't drive to—Baltimore. He went grocery shopping."

"True. Last week I forgot Jonesy's vet appointment. It happens."

Rose recognizes June's comment as disingenuously upbeat but accepts it as the answer she wants. There's no point in challenging the equivalence of June's analogy, especially if it makes her feel more comfortable with the situation. *After all*, Rose thinks, *how much decrepitude can June handle before beating a full retreat to the vitality of her own life? And poor Kel. It must be even worse for him.*

"I'm sure he feels—badly enough about it," Rose says. "No sense making an issue. But please—watch him. There's only so much—I see."

June's smile is characteristically reassuring. "Of course," she says.

# FIELD RESEARCH

*Tuesday, May 5*

Kelsey is at his window admiring the spring and imagining Rose in it. Alternating rain and sun have thickened the various greens and added new colors. Rose has continued to rally. The longer, warmer days, cutting back on painkillers and almost daily visits from Mrs. Danhill have reanimated her. She is eager to make the trip to the deck for meals and sun baths. On her best days she is able to maneuver herself out of bed and make it to the deck on her own with Coleridge or Dostoevsky or Rilke or McCarthy and her bell in tow. Kelsey allows himself to believe that with a little extra TLC and encouragement she might find motivation and stamina enough to make it to the stairlift for dinner in the dining room, something they haven't tried since last fall. She may even take a brief garden tour of the back yard. Who knows? It's something to work toward.

Outside, Mrs. Danhill emerges carrying her dog and two canvas shopping bags. She places the bags in her rear bicycle basket, her dog in her handlebar basket, and rides off for her regular trip to the farmer's market. As she disappears from view, it occurs to Kelsey how little he really knows about her. She and Rose have become friendly, but her visits are often while he is away or otherwise engaged. Rose shares little of what they discuss, says there's nothing to tell. Reminiscing, Rose calls it. Mrs. Danhill apparently misses her son and grandchildren and spends a lot of time on church activities. Kelsey laments that his interactions with Mrs. Danhill are superficial. He doesn't know her interests, her taste in art, books, music, the name of her son, or, oddly enough, even her dog. He doesn't know what sort of home a proper, independent if somewhat gullible god-fearing woman keeps. Is she tidy or a hoarder? If she has magazines

lying around, which ones? Are there flea market finds on her
mantel or Steuben Art Glass? Does she drink? What does she
fear? Rose volunteers none of this.

There's a way he can know what even Rose does not. If he
could breach the prophylactic walls preempting their natural
tribal bonding, he could learn what can only be learned through
careful observation of the subject in its habitat. Custom dictates
that he wait for an invitation, so if he is to gain access, he needs
to devise some pretext, some natural prelude to *Please come in.*
A gift or perhaps something to borrow. Borrow seems best.
She'd invite him inside while she finds…what? It's too soon for
anything from her garden. Something from her kitchen would
allow deeper access to the various chambers of her domicile.

"Good god, listen to me," he says to the window. "What
is this plotting, this lunacy? She's my neighbor, very nearly a
friend. What am I thinking?"

Rose sits up tall in her elevated bed. Too distracted by her
thoughts, she sets aside the crossword puzzle she's having trouble cracking and turns to her father. *So, Dad, cutting back on those
little white pills has lifted the veil. I can think again and this is what I
think. I've learned about loss, no thanks to you. A person becomes whole
not despite loss but because of it. Loss becomes a part of you and fills holes
created by want, expectation, time. Loss reminds us that what we are right
now is complete. It doesn't matter what we think we're missing. We aren't
missing anything that couldn't be taken away and still leave us whole, only
different. There's less of me every day, but I'm more complete for it. More
complete? No, that's wrong. There aren't degrees of completeness, only this
completeness and the next completeness. Completeness doesn't depend on
whether we recognize it. Name it. Completeness just is. So-called seekers
are just clueless morons who haven't smacked their foreheads on this truth
yet. The truth doesn't need them to discover it, to acknowledge it. This isn't
a believe-it-or-not proposition as far as the natural world is concerned.
There's only accept it or not. Period. The kicker is that some idiots think
embracing this fucked-up truth will bring them peace. Ha! Accepting that
this doomed skin is the only skin you get and being comfortable knowing*

*that—I mean really comfortable, your kind of comfortable—is rare. Like albino alligator rare. We put on our skin and then scratch at it our entire, pitiful lives hoping we can shed it and grow a new one. Not you, Daddio. You didn't just accept your own skin, you actually enjoyed your own company. Whoever you were at any moment was just fine with you. And whoever or whatever came along to rattle your atoms and change things up a bit, well, that was okay, too. So why couldn't you teach me, you selfish son-of-a-bitch? Why'd you keep it to yourself? My skin's turning to atoms before my eyes, breaking away bit by bit. I'm turning to dust and I'm still scratching. You bastard. Why didn't you teach me?*

❧

Until this very moment June has never seen Alice out walking Prince. She always assumed Alice's tennis ball routine in the carport was her way of exercising her dog. She sits on the bottom step of the stoop of her side porch smoking a cigarette and tossing the ball against the chain-link fence. Half the time Prince anticipates her feeble toss, snags the ball out of the air and drops it back at her feet before she can take her next drag. But today they are actually out for a walk.

"Hi, Alice. This is a first."

Alice rolls her eyes and sucks on her cigarette. "Yeah, I've got dog duty. Rob hurt his ankle."

"I'm sorry to hear that."

"Ah, it's nothing," she says through a cloud of smoke. "He's just being a big baby about it."

"At least we've got lovely weather," June says.

"Yeah, it'd be great if dipstick here didn't try to dislocate my shoulder every time he sees a squirrel."

June laughs politely. "Look at him perk up when you say squirrel."

"The genius wouldn't know what to do with one if he caught it." Alice draws on her cigarette. "So, I see you in and out of the Geddes's place," Alice says. "What's that about?"

For a second June experiences the sensation—a sort of heartburn—that comes with being caught doing something she thought was private. She has lived next door to Rose for twenty years and they have barely said boo to one another. Now, as Rose is dying, it is as if they have formed a sisterhood based on comparing their losses. The *sotto voce* murmurings of grief, Rose calls it, what they each would admit only to themselves if June hadn't stumbled onto the confessional that is Rose's deck. Sharing any of this with Alice feels like a violation of a trust. So instead June says, "Professor Geddes and I have been talking about getting some work done on the property between our houses. We have trees and vines in common."

"Uh-huh," Alice says, nods and takes another pull on her cigarette. "So, how's Rose doin'?"

June decides reporting on Rose's condition is not a breach of confidence. She tells Alice about the way Rose has rallied over the last few weeks. A pill that goes after the tumors that turned up in her brain seems to be helping. And cutting back on her painkillers has made her feel more alert. "She seems," June says, "to have developed a renewed interest in trying to enjoy these last months." Rose knows, June is quick to point out, that feeling better doesn't mean a whole lot when you're dealing with stage-four lung cancer.

Alice drops the last of her cigarette in the street and grinds it under her foot. Prince sniffs at it and she jerks his leash. "Leave it, numb-nuts. Stupid dog. Well, give Rose my best. I'd drop by myself but I'm no good with sickness like that. Gives me the willies."

"I understand. It's not pretty," June says, hoping to reinforce Alice's squeamishness, and then changes the subject. "Other than the ankle, how's Rob?"

❧

The church bells chime five. Kelsey is in his front yard half-heartedly harvesting the bindweed that has wrapped itself around the hydrangeas when it comes to him. Basil. Fresh basil. This morning he saw a prodigious bunch among June's farmer's market bounty. It makes perfect sense. He decides to try to catch her before she takes her dog for his evening walk.

As he crosses June's front porch, he looks in the living

room windows. June isn't downstairs, at least not where he can see her. He knocks on the door. There's no barking or movement. He opens the screen and knocks directly on the wooden door. Still no response. Must have just missed them. On impulse he tries the knob. It's unlocked. *More evidence of her naiveté,* he thinks. *Her misplaced trust.*

He opens the door and sticks his head in. "Hello?" he calls. No response. "Mrs. Danhill, it's Kelsey Geddes." Still nothing.

Given her routine, he can't have missed her by much. He decides he'll wait on the porch. The smell of baking, something sweet with a hint of cinnamon, is a hospitable surprise. He lingers a moment to take in the scent and the view from the entryway. Details. He admires the bouquet on the Shaker sofa table and the half-assembled songbird jigsaw puzzle on her glass coffee table—not nearly as daunting as Rose's bookshelf puzzle. Mrs. Danhill's long-haired cat looks like a fur hat balled up in the bay window. It doesn't even acknowledge his presence.

On the coatrack behind the door hangs a khaki utility vest and expensive-looking binoculars. *Is there a man I've missed?* The living room is unnaturally neat. The dog's wishbone-shaped chew toy in the middle of the floor is the only thing in the room that seems out of its prescribed place, and even the toy's random locus seems somehow intentional. There are three photos on the fireplace mantel, two that include Mr. Danhill, along with a pair of decorative candles and a wood carving of hummingbirds drinking from bell-shaped flowers. Above the mantel is a large framed print of two cranes or herons, he doesn't remember the difference. Their imperial postures suggest they are rulers of the marsh they wade in.

Simple, it all says. Unassuming and quiet. But, he realizes, he is drawing conclusions. Research begins with gathering data, attention to details. Conclusions come later. His instincts tell him the more interesting details will be upstairs, in the less public corridors and rooms. He climbs with the cautious deliberation not of an intruder, but of a guest who does not want to disturb anyone or anything, though even ruffling the air, he is well aware, can leave a telltale mark. He must move through this world with confident care, as if he belongs.

It's difficult, as every detail reminds him that this is not his natural environment. Multiple tiers of family photographs line the staircase. Kids. Kids and parents. Various instars of nymphs and their adults fill the wall. A menagerie from a collective memory. The black-and-white pictures are perhaps grandparents. There's the young Mrs. Danhill. Barely changed today. Her hair now a bit lighter. A little more flesh. Her thorax and abdomen squarer now. Details.

He climbs and navigates the corridors to the sleeping chamber. It is precisely what the main living chamber has prepared him for: immaculate order. The only piece of clothing out of place is a midnight-blue cashmere pullover lying on the bed. A layer she must have decided she didn't need for the walk. But, again, he's drawing conclusions. *Just look,* he reminds himself. *See the details.* The bed itself is neatly made up with a bold flower print motif. Large white lilies on a sun-yellow field spill onto the floor on both sides of the faux-antique, sleigh-style frame. The six pillows of three different sizes and three different pillowcase patterns look like a catalog photo shoot arrangement.

Most of the furniture appears to be of a set, including the two side tables and a dresser with an attached mirror. The only piece that does not match is the corner vanity, also dark wood but without the same floral detail on the drawer face and knobs. This is where she sits to brush her hair. The gleaming silver-plated vintage brush is surprisingly heavy. He imagines it practically pulling itself through her hair. There are two jars of cream, one for face, one for hands. The dog's bed is beside her vanity. He was certain the dog shared her bed. *This is why field research is so important.*

The room is largely free of extraneous accoutrements. On top of her dresser are a cherry-stained jewelry box, a photo of her with, he assumes, her parents, taken against a backdrop of a

European city, a wedding photograph of her and her husband, and a brass trinket tray containing a single earring, lip balm, three dimes, a nickel, and two pennies.

The alarm clock on her bedside table clicks over to the next minute.

He makes his way to the grooming area. Here his impression is that she lets her guard down a bit, or maybe her hair down is more apropos. Though not messy, neither is the room pin neat. A couple of articles of clothing are tossed onto rather than into the wicker hamper. A used washcloth is draped over the side of the sink. A long, auburn hair runs across the oval bowl like a thin crack. Oddly, the toothpaste cap is missing. Various body lotions and creams are scattered about the countertop. She recently used one that has left behind a faint and familiar scent of coconut. Two hand-washed bras are draped over the glass shower door. Notably, they are not pristine white or dull flesh tones, but colors. One black, one teal. And satin soft, almost plush to the touch. Both embroidered with lace. *Does Our Lady of the Prim Exterior conceal a secret naughtiness? A bit of color under her wings?* His ears warm with the flush of… of what? *Let it go. This is not about the observer. Focus on the observed.*

With some trepidation, he opens the medicine cabinet. He is relieved to discover that she is not a sneaky slob. The inside is orderly, the only surprise here being prescription pill vials: unfinished two-year-old Vicodin and a more recent one labeled BuSpar, a drug he doesn't recognize. Another valuable detail. His research is paying off handsomely.

The linen closet is also in reasonable order, though she does have a catchall basket on the bottom shelf filled with an uncharacteristically random collection of paraphernalia. He riffles through the emery boards, empty travel-sized bottles, loose buttons and Band-Aids, cosmetic and perfume samples, eyelash curler, hair clips, lipsticks, and fingernail clippers. All the way at the bottom he notices what appears to be a small pocketknife. More a novelty than a useful tool. Small and silver, it is essentially a keyring with a tiny knife blade, a scissor, and a nail file that appears to double as a screwdriver. It's a minor detail of little significance, certainly not relevant to the environmental balance of the domain. He slips it into his front pants pocket, an excavated memento of his research.

Backing out he checks to see that he hasn't obviously disturbed anything. It is critical that the observer not leave any trace that might influence the subsequent behavior of the observed. Cabinet and closet doors closed. No discernable impressions in the carpet. He turns at the top of the stairs and begins his descent.

Voices. He freezes. Laughter and light conversation from the front of the house. Mrs. Danhill is talking to the woman from across the street. His first instinct is to go out to meet them, to share the fruits of his findings. But there is a second thought, a thought accompanied by panic. The sudden awareness that he doesn't belong here. That he must leave. Must gather his wits and move quickly. He stays as close to the wall as he can without disturbing the pictures. He descends one meticulous step at a time. At the first floor landing he drops to his hands and knees. The cat lifts its head and pricks its ears but stays put. He scrambles through the living room toward the back door. He makes the kitchen just as the oven timer starts beeping and Mrs. Danhill's steps creak across the front porch. The front door opens as he's leaving through the back. He covers his exit by knocking on the door as he pulls it closed.

Jonesy barks in response to a knock on the back door and strains at his leash. The knock startles June as much as it does the dog. No one ever comes to their back door. She holds tight to the leash and tries to see who it is from the living room. Professor Geddes turns around and starts smiling and waving like she has caught him playing some prank. *What an odd man*, she thinks. He's smiling, so she doesn't imagine it's bad news. She takes a moment to compose herself and unhook Jonesy's leash before opening the door.

"Hello, Professor, is everything all right?"

"Oh yes, fine," he says and pauses. He seems to be picking

his next words carefully. "One of these days, I'm going to convince you to call me Kelsey."

June's pretty sure this isn't why he's standing on her back porch, but she plays along. "Okay," she says. "How about when you stop calling me Mrs. Danhill?"

"How would you prefer I address you?"

"How about June?" she says, assuming this is all part of some droll game he's concocted.

"Yes, of course. Good."

To June, Kelsey seems a bit irrationally pleased with the exchange, as if some grand accord has been reached.

"Well, Mrs.—June," he stutters. "I'm sorry. It seems so forward, and yet I feel we've known one another for so long."

At this point June can't keep from smiling. His boyish awkwardness is almost silly. She would laugh, but she can tell he's not kidding. "I'm sure you'll get used to it," she says. When he just stands there with a dim-witted grin, she adds, "Is that really why you came over?"

"No, no," he says, snapping out of his reverie. "There was just something about hearing you call me Professor that struck me as oddly impersonal. I don't know why. Forgive the digression. I've actually come to beg a favor. I'm wondering if you have any fresh basil I can con you out of. I'm preparing a dish for Rose and, unhappily, my basil's salad days are over. I was hoping to avoid a run to the store for just a few leaves."

"Sure. I picked some up this morning. Come in."

It relaxes June to have Kelsey mention Rose. Her addition to the conversation diminishes the queer flirtatiousness she was beginning to pick up on. She is sure she's just projecting, but she hasn't seen this sort of social clumsiness from the professor since his first conversation with the Mem Park boys. Then again, he's never asked a favor of her.

"Something smells good," he says.

"We're baking pies for a sale over at the church."

"We?"

"Jonesy likes to believe he helps."

Jonesy sniffs the professor's shoes and pant legs. Kelsey doesn't seem to notice.

"You have a lovely home," he says.

"Is this the first time you've seen it?"

"But for a glimpse from the front door, yes."

"Hard to believe after all these years," June says. She holds out a small bunch of basil. "Here you go. Is this enough?"

"More than. Thank you." He performs a stately bow and turns to leave.

"Please tell Rose I'll come by tomorrow after all. I told her I might not make it until Thursday, but my plans changed."

"She'll be delighted to hear that."

June closes the door behind him and bends over to remove Jonesy's harness.

"What do you think, Jonesy? Time to start worrying about the professor? I'm beginning to see what Rose means. Help me keep an eye on him, okay? Now, what do you say we get these pies out before we burn them."

⁂

The shrill resolve of a seemingly endless *dingdingdingding* shoots another spasm of panic through his body. The metallic scream pulls him up the stairs two at a time. He bursts heroically into the room and sings, "Here I am to save the day—"

Rose has the head of the bed raised. Her hand is draped over the bell. Her eyes are closed, her mouth open, her empty pill tray in her lap.

"Rose?" he whispers. He lifts her hand to check her pulse. Her eyes flare open.

"Where were you?" The words leap from her tongue like flames. "I have been ringing!" she wails.

That she is capable of such anger is encouraging. She's alive. Fuming with life. "I'm here, dear," he says. "I just stepped outside. I was weeding. The bindweed is celebrating your absence."

"Dropped my pills. Need a pill. It hurts."

"Your script is my command."

"Oh, shut up," she hisses.

The sting of her reproach quiets him. Her pills are scattered under the bed and across the floor. He crawls around and collects what he can find, distributing them among the seven slots in the pill tray. "Here you are, dear. I'll get you some fresh water."

Returning with the refilled glass, he sits in silence until her body relaxes back into its sepulchral state. After several minutes she says, in her normal half-voice, "Thank you."

"Of course," he says. "I'm sorry I was late."

Her face lolls toward him. "Mighty Mouse?" she sneers.

"Too much?" he asks, with a contrite knitting of his brow.

"Who does that make me, Pearl Blackheart?"

"That's funny."

She sighs heavily. "I'm sorry I'm dying," she says.

"As well you should be," Kelsey says, and cradles her hand in his. "But not quite yet, please."

"You can't seriously—want me around—like this."

"I can't imagine what I'd do without you."

She grins ghoulishly as ever. "Such a gallant liar."

"I wish I were lying. You'd think after years of preparation I'd be at least as ready as you are for this, your adjustment to what's next being, well, somewhat more irreversible than anything I might dream up for myself."

Rose glares at him as if he's speaking nonsense. "Do you really not see it?" she asks.

He glances around the room, taking a quick inventory to make sure whatever she's referring to is not staring him in the face. "See what, dear?"

"Your journey, too, is—irreversible."

He breaks eye contact, not wanting her to see his involuntary welling. He knows she hates banal sentiment. He looks at her hands. He tries to rub them back to life with his thumbs. He blinks repeatedly. Sniffs surreptitiously. She misses nothing.

"It's okay," she says. "I know those tears are—for you. You mercifully stopped—weeping for me—ages ago."

*My thick-thorned Rose. My briar Rose. A bramble to keep her prince in. She possesses me. Our grief binds us.* When she began her slow wilt, he was drawn to her more strongly. To him, her weakness is a sort of glamour. He is at once repulsed by her personification of death and drawn to the memory of what dwells beneath her morbid disguise. She is his journey's end and the beginning, all those years ago in a field with butterfly nets in ecstatic pursuit of the rare and elusive *Callophrys gryneus*. She is the olfactory affront of decay and the intoxicating citrus of her favorite namesake, the lemon-yellow Radiant Perfume Grandiflora. He is the willing victim of her sway, even when on bad days he imagines this life, his devotion, a form of suicide. All of this he believes but will never tell her. There is no need. She, he is certain, already knows.

He says, "Tears for me, maybe, but always from you."

Rose manages a mocking pout and says, "You know I dislike—vulgar romanticism—as much as—sentimentality."

He wipes his eyes. "Forgive me," he says. "I don't know what overcame me."

"If you weren't such a—soppy dope, I might just—fall in love with you."

"If you weren't such a thorny flower, I might just pick you too."

She huffs a feeble laugh and says, "Too late now."

Kelscy leans over and kisses her bloodless lips, runs the backs of his fingers across the cool, fine fabric of her cheek.

He leaves her sleeping sitting up and returns to his study. When he sits down, he senses a small object in his pocket. He traces the shape through the khaki. When it reminds him of nothing he would expect to find there, he reaches in and retrieves it. It's a silver pocketknife. There's nothing remarkable about it, except that it's not his. He notices there are initials on one side: D.A.D. The engraving infuses the ornamental object with a power that generates heat. He drops it on the desk and rubs his fingertips.

*What have I done?*

# A CONSPIRACY

*Thursday, May 7*

*Hey, Daddio, I hope you noticed I made my own way out to the balcony again today. It took some doing, but I made it without splintering into a million pieces. I'm actually feeling pretty good, thanks for asking.*

Rose sits at the sunflower table waiting for June. She loves this time of year. The delicate time. The first clutches of baby birds will be hatching soon. Spring babies remind her of the heartrending howls of the neighborhood vixen back in December. She woke Rose with a horrible heat-sparked shriek. She was either looking for a mate or was already humping. Hard to tell the difference.

Rose had responded to the fox's plaint by telling Kel she misses sex. He started in for about the hundredth time with how exciting it was for him that she had so shamelessly expressed her pleasure. Not just sex, he's always quick to add, but all pleasure: a particularly good Bolognese sauce, a hot bath, the scent of fresh cut lilacs, anything Vivaldi, a long, desert horseback ride under a clear night sky…a mostly accurate list of things that elicit her sighs, moans, gasps. He's right. She never suffered pleasure's *Sturm und Drang* in silence. To emote is to give thanks. Monosyllabic prayers to no deity in particular, just expressions of gratitude for her five senses and the natural world's ability to thrill them.

Her dad used to say, "We humans have a finite capacity to indulge in the world's infinite gifts. Once you've exhausted that capacity, you're either really boring or dead, and I'm not interested in either of those states of being."

*I miss it all,* Rose says. *Every crumb, whiff, hue. I'm not afraid to die. I know you think I am, but it's not that. I still miss it. Don't want to let it go. When will I be ready? Well, it comes down to the contest between*

*pain and pleasure. As much as I love my pleasures, I'm no fan of this*
*pain. I just can't stand the idea of pain winning. If my expressions of*
*pleasure are my little prayers, then my responses to pain are unholy curses,*
*howls, tantrums. Staying alive is my final tantrum. But I don't want to go*
*kicking and screaming. I want to go out on the wings of one of my little*
*prayers, grinning smugly at the caped concierge as he ushers me down that*
*dark hallway. I wish I could draw a hard line like you did. Just say today's*
*the day. But I don't have your certainty. I keep thinking I'm going to miss*
*out on something grand. One more difference between us that I failed to*
*recognize.*

Rose allows her dad to drift away and relaxes back in her
chair. Today she feels pretty good about where she's sitting on
the pleasure-pain continuum. A thin veil of clouds dulls the
sky's blue, but not her mood. She hears the back gate open and
close and her mood brightens further with anticipation. She's
made a new friend of sorts, or perhaps more accurately an ally.
Either way, her world is one person bigger. June's guilelessness
and agreeability, her wholesome Christian optimism may all
mix into a personality as beige as her complexion, but she's
close and available. In younger days, Rose probably would have
hidden in a meat locker rather than hang out with someone like
June. Maggie, if she met June, would likely elbow Rose and ask,
"Where'd you find the nun?" But Rose has come to appreciate
that diers can't be choosers. After nearly five decades of life
with Kel, she's developed, if not genuine patience, at least a
selective forbearance. June, she finds, is someone for whom she
is able to make allowances.

As if on cue, June enters the bedroom empty-handed.

"No tea today?" Rose asks.

June rests her hands on the back of a café table chair and
gives Rose an uncharacteristically mischievous look. "You seem
pretty comfortable making your own way out here to the deck,"
June says. "So, I thought we might try something different today."

Rose isn't sure she's up for *different* but she's curious enough
to ask, "What exactly do you—have in mind?"

"I thought we might have tea down on the patio."

Rose works through the implications of the suggestion. A walk down the hall. The stairlift to the first floor. A straight shot down the center hall to the lower door opening onto the patio would avoid having to make her way through the dining room, kitchen, and down the back-porch steps. Once out of the center hall, it's only ten or maybe fifteen feet to the wicker chairs. Sitting comfortably on her balcony, the prospect of relocating strikes her as unnecessarily onerous, but doable. June's enthusiasm sways her. Disappointing June might discourage future visits. Rose wouldn't want June to start thinking of her as an old woman dying of cancer.

"Sounds like great fun," Rose says. To punctuate her commitment to the challenge, she lifts herself from her chair at the sunflower table before June can come around to help.

"Here, let me get that—"

"I'm fine," Rose insists. She gathers her oxygen and cane and strikes off toward the bedroom door.

June falls in behind her. "Careful," she says. "Not too fast now."

"Not my problem if—you can't keep up."

After so many months of convalescence, Rose imagines the feeling of stepping out into the hallway as being like how an astronaut must feel after returning from months on the space station. The house suddenly feels so large. Both familiar and new. The air is lighter in the hallway, as are the wall colors. Being indoors outside of her bedroom is as uplifting as being outside on the deck. She silently scolds herself for having holed up for so long.

At the top of the stairs she says to June, "You take my cane. I'll manage the tank." Rose sits on the stairlift and June lays the oxygen across her lap. "I'll race you," Rose says, and pushes the power button. The chair begins to glide down the rail.

"It's so quiet," June says.

"And so slow. I used to be tempted—to ride the bannister."

June laughs. "That I'd like to see."

"Me too."

June passes Rose on the landing as the lift makes the

one-hundred-eighty-degree arc to start down the second flight
of stairs. At the bottom, she helps Rose out of the lift and
returns her cane. Rose takes the lead into the center hall and
toward the back door.

"I love your house," June says. "The formal dining room and
the big living room. Is the tiling around the fireplace the same
artist who did your table?"

"It is. She's very talented—"

"When she's sober," June says with a laugh.

"Oh, damn. I'm repeating myself."

"I'm sorry, I—"

"Not at all," Rose interrupts. "Please stop me. Nothing more
tedious—than an old lady—repeating her old jokes."

Rose waits for June to open the back door so she can maneuver around it in the narrow hallway. She hesitates before
taking the slight step down from the threshold to the patio.

"You're doing great," June says. Rose senses both happiness
and relief in her voice.

"Don't know why—I haven't tried this. Kel let me—convince myself—I couldn't."

"I have a confession to make," June says. "This wasn't my
idea. Kelsey asked if I would encourage you because it's such
a nice day. He's stopping at the bakery to pick up croissants on
his way back from the barber. Our tea is steeping."

"A conspiracy," Rose groans. "I've been duped."

"I didn't exactly twist your arm."

"Thank you for that," Rose says, and stops to look around
at the freshly planted patio pots that have been arranged in the
seating area. "Look what you've done," she says. "They're quite
beautiful."

"I thought it would be a bit much to ask you to walk all the
way out to the back garden, so I thought I'd bring a little of the
garden to the patio."

"Thank you. Pots haven't looked—this good in years. The
creeping jenny is—nice touch."

"I appreciate you saying so. I've always admired your pots. I
just hoped to do them justice."

"You done good. Now, where's the old man?"

"I'm sure he'll be here any minute. I'm going to check on the tea. Can I get you anything?"

"No, I'll wait. Just hope whatever he brings—is as good as your cookies."

"Ah, that's sweet. I'll be right back."

Rose watches June disappear into the house, then closes her eyes and does a quick assessment of her body. The effort has left her feeling both proud of herself and a little beat up. The places that ache are the same, just a bit noisier. Showing off for June tired her more than she anticipated. In the future, she'll remember to approach these adventures less recklessly. *In the future…* The phrase amuses her. What hubris to believe she has anything resembling a future. *Oh, Daddio, I know the only future I have is with you. And I know you begrudge me dragging out the inevitable. Allow me my choice. You made yours. You begged for the end. I'm not there yet.*

"I'm sorry, Rose. What was that?"

Rose opens her eyes and June is setting the serving platter with the tea pot and cups down on the coffee table.

"Were you talking to me?" June asks.

"No. Sorry. Muttering to myself. A little death rattle. Like passing gas."

June smiles. "You're a piece of work, Mrs. Geddes."

The driveway gravel signals Kel's return. "About time," Rose says. "He must have been—flirting with his hairdresser."

"Stop that," June says. "Your husband is a perfect gentleman."

"Now you're repeating yourself," Rose says. "Hardly perfect. But close enough."

Kelsey comes through the gate with guns blazing. "I know. I'm late. *Un migliaio di scuse.* I was halfway home before I remembered the bakery and then there was actually a line on a Thursday afternoon."

June raises her hands to calm him. It's a gesture that has

carried over from the classroom. She catches herself, lowers her hands, and, using her indoor voice, says, "It's fine, Professor. We've only been out here a few minutes."

She's relieved when Kelsey is reassured rather than reacting as if she'd shushed him like an overwrought child. "Ah, then perfect timing," he says. "The croissants are still warm."

He hands the bag to June and she arranges the rolls on the platter.

"Now it's a party," Rose says.

"Yes, it is," Kelsey agrees, as he pulls the chair next to Rose within reach of the coffee table. "And in that party spirit, I brought almond, chocolate, and pastry cream-filled."

Rose is unimpressed. "And plain, I hope. I want mine with—butter and—raspberry preserves."

Using his hand rather than the tongs June placed on the platter, Kelsey picks out the plain croissant, drops it on Rose's plate and says, "Then plain with butter and raspberry preserves you shall have."

"Butter's here," June says. "Are the preserves in the refrigerator or the pantry?"

"I believe there is an open jar in the fridge," Kelsey says. "You stay. I'll go."

When Kelsey is gone, Rose signals for June to huddle in closer. "Does he seem a bit—over the top to you?"

June has resigned herself to this being the way it is every time the three of them visit together: Rose looking to June to validate her suspicions regarding the professor's behavior. *What can I say?* June thinks. *Yes, the professor is eccentric and theatrical and silly. But hasn't he always been? Is this really new behavior? I doubt it. But I haven't been married to him for forty-something years, so who am I to judge him as any more or less eccentric or theatrical or silly than he has been for all that time?* June steps back, smiles at Rose, and says, "I think he's behaving like a man who loves his wife and knows the two of you don't have much time left. If that means he occasionally goes over the top, well, so be it."

June reads Rose's puzzled look as a processing of information rather than confusion. Rose seems to be working out an equation that calculates meaning based on word choice, inflection, and physical demeanor. "What?" June asks.

After a moment, Rose says, "You like him."

June's shoulders sag under the weight not of what is said but of what is implied. "Yes," she says, "of course I do. He's a very nice man."

"You like him."

"Rose," June says, drawing out the single syllable and raising her intonation in a way that once signaled to naughty children that she was on to them. "What are you doing?"

Rose's grin is probably intended to be mischievous, but it reads as menacing.

Kelsey's return with the jam interrupts them. "Here you are, my sweet." When the two women look back at each other rather than engaging with him, he asks, "What did I miss?"

"Nothing," June jumps in. "We're picking up right where you left. The tea is ready and the croissants warm."

Kelsey watches Rose slowly go to work on her roll. "Would you like me to cut that open for you?"

"I'm weak—but I think I can still—manage a croissant."

"Suit yourself. It's great to see you down here on the patio going toe to toe with that thing. Vegas has the odds at even, but I'm betting on you to butter and jam that rascal."

Rose says to June, "See what I've had to—live with for—forty-seven years."

June resists the urge to call them cute. "I imagine," she says, "it's been a very entertaining half-century."

A broad smile animates Kelsey's features. "There have been lots of laughs, right, dear?"

Rose chuckles. "Joni Mitchell," she says.

Kelsey looks at June. June shrugs her confusion.

"Acid, booze, and ass," Rose says. She gets no help from the others. "Blue," she prompts.

"Sorry," June says, "I don't know it."

Rose looks at Kelsey. "Needles, guns, and grass…"

"I'm sorry, dear, I don't follow."

"That's your cue."

Kelsey is lost. "My cue?"

Rose drops her hands into her lap in exasperation. "I'm being entertained by—a couple of cultural illiterates." Rose waves her knife like a baton and counts out, "Acid, booze, ass. Needles, guns, grass, and..." She points the knife at Kelsey.

"Lots of laughs?" June offers.

Rose cackles. "Lots of laughs."

Kelsey's spirits don't seem to be affected by his failure to sync up with Rose or by June's ability to make the connection he couldn't. He smiles at his wife's amusement and reaches for the chocolate croissant. "Rose," he explains to June, "was much more of a counterculture music fan than I. What little musical taste I have ranges from the Baroque to the Romantic."

"Mitchell is a romantic," Rose says, as she reunites the halves of her croissant.

"And now," Kelsey says, "you see what I have had to live with for forty-seven years."

June laughs and tells them they seem like the perfect match to her.

The visit goes on much like this until the tea and rolls are gone. The process of preparing and consuming her croissant and tea seems to have spent Rose. June reloads the tea tray. Kelsey goes with her to the house to hold the door. June asks him to join her in the kitchen. She has a question.

"Just before you got back," June says, "when I was setting the tea out, I heard Rose talking to someone, or so I thought. It sounded like she said, 'You begged for the end.' When I asked her, she dismissed it. Said she was just muttering to herself. It was a little disturbing. Does it make any sense to you?"

"Sadly, it does," Kelsey says. "When she decided to stop all treatments except the pills, she started talking to her dead father."

"Oh," June says, thinking she understands. "Her way of preparing, I guess. But... 'You begged for the end'? His death must have been horrible."

"Hmm, well, I wasn't there," Kelsey says. "She was. He was a very active, independent, proud, and rather difficult man before his stroke. She went out to move him from the hospital back to his home. The prognosis for recovery was bleak and a long convalescence. That wasn't an option for her father. Swallowed his entire bottle of painkillers. I imagine that's what they were discussing when you stumbled into the conversation."

"That's awful. It must have been so hard on her."

"Became harder after the charges."

"Charges?"

"Assisted suicide. A felony. Nasty business."

June is confused. She works through Kelsey's words but can't bring herself to understand their meaning. "What are you saying?" she asks.

"Her father asked for his pills," he explains. "Rose handed him the bottle and a glass of water. He did the rest."

June tries to picture the scene. Her only point of reference is the man in the photograph on Rose's bedside table. She can't imagine him ending his own life. Her image is of a man who would cling to life with whatever strength remained. He would defy his doctor's prognosis and confound his rehabilitation team with the speed and extent of his recovery. He would declare his intention to live to a hundred. "I just can't believe it," June says.

"It took a year, but the judge finally dismissed the case."

"How did I not know about this?"

"Happened out west. Thankfully, it wasn't news here."

June takes a deep breath and attempts to push the scene out of her mind. "I'm so sorry," she says. "It's none of my business."

"Not to worry," Kelsey reassures her. "Ancient history."

"I should be going. Is there anything else I can do?"

Kelsey tells her he can handle the trip back upstairs when Rose is ready. They return to the porch to find Rose sleeping in her chair.

June turns to Kelsey and says in a hushed tone, "Enjoy the rest of your day."

"Don't forget to—water the flowerpots," Rose says, without opening her eyes.

Kelsey laughs. "She's ordering you around now. That's a good sign. She only abuses those she loves."

June smiles a gentle scold at Kelsey. "I don't think that quite qualifies as abuse," she says.

"In time, dear," Rose says. "In time."

⬦

Back upstairs Rose seems more than ready for her afternoon nap. As Kelsey tucks her in, he says, "I think that was quite a successful experiment. I'm impressed, my frail darling."

"I must confess, there was a bit of— showing off. Hate June to think of me as—the dying old lady."

Kelsey laughs. "Whatever would give her that idea?"

Rose lies back on her pillows and closes her eyes. Kelsey kicks off his shoes and cuddles in next to her without getting under the covers. He is not interested in napping just now and doesn't want to disturb her when he leaves the room.

"Mrs. Danhill is a lovely person," he says. Rose's eyes crack open just enough so he can see she is not yet asleep. "And she seemed to enjoy herself," he adds. "I don't think you have to worry about her thinking of you as a dying old woman. She seemed quite engaged."

"She likes you," Rose says, almost inaudibly.

"Well, I hope so. I wouldn't want to be an impediment to her visiting you. She's had a very positive effect on you."

Kelsey stops himself from adding that he enjoys June's company as well; that he feels she has brought life back into a house that has been shrouded in mourning for too long. He knows better. Rose will want him to explain exactly what it is he is feeling. Especially after today's escapade. She will assume that he and June have been meeting and plotting in secret and that today was just one of many schemes. She would never accept his explanation that this was an idea hatched in the driveway as he was going to get his haircut. He knew June was coming for a visit later. She was in her backyard when he went to the car. He suggested the idea. June said she was fine with it if Rose was, and that was that. But, he is certain, that would not be that for Rose.

Her lips twitch again, but no sound comes out. When he is sure she is asleep, he slips off the bed and goes to his office. He has a new angle he is exploring for his paper.

# Mother's Day

*Sunday, May 10*

Kel folds his section of the *New York Times* in half and tilts the picture of a breaching orca toward Rose. "This is a sad story," he says.

She looks up from her crossword puzzle. "Do I want to hear it?"

"Maybe not."

"But you want to share."

"It's up to you."

"Give me a hint."

"It's about a mother orca."

"And?"

"Her baby died."

"That's it?"

"She grieved for seventeen days."

"Grieved? An orca?"

"That's the point of the story. She carried her dead baby girl a thousand miles before letting her go. After growing inside her mother for a year and a half, the calf lived for just thirty minutes. The mother balanced her dead daughter on her head and swam up and down the Salish Sea, diving into the darkness to retrieve the calf whenever it slipped off."

"That is sad," Rose says.

"At one point, the other mothers formed a circle around her. They sang to her, soothed her. Eventually she was able to release her daughter."

"Hmm," Rose says. She returns to her puzzle but wonders to herself if the mother orca believed in miracles? Does she have an omniscient, benevolent orcan power she prays to and in which she places an irrational faith; one she trusts would never inflict such fierce pain on a subject as faithful and obedient as she? And has her loss shaken her faith in her omniscient? Strengthened her trust in her sisterhood? *No one circled around me. No one sang songs to release my sorrow so it could drift in perfect peace to the bottom of the world. But then mine was a lima bean. Less human than a mama orca's baby. Did I even grieve? Do I still?*

Kel says, "Sorry to interrupt your puzzling."

"Hmm," Rose says.

❧

"The bouquet my son sent me," June explains, "is bigger than any of my vases can handle, so I divided it and brought half to you."

"I don't qualify," Rose says.

June places the bouquet on the sunflower table. "Just sharing the wealth," she says. "Spreading the joy. I know you'll appreciate them." She fluffs the flowers and adds, "You've never told me about yours."

"Mine?"

"Your mother."

"My mother?"

"Yes," June says. She removes one broken stem, pinches it off at the appropriate length and threads it through Rose's hat band. "I don't mean to pry, but your mother's absence in your life story is so conspicuous."

"Conspicuous absence," Rose says under her breath, and thinks, *If she only knew how appropriate her casual observation is. Mom was here and then gone and then me and my dad were gone and then Mom was farther away…and all the time I thought I was somehow the cause of all the distance, all the going. Dad insisted that leaving was my mother's thing. He told me he couldn't remember a time when my mother was actually with him, even when they were together in the same room. He said it was one of the things that attracted him to her. Her flyaway personality absolved him of any responsibility to be where she was. By the time he'd get there, the slightest shift in the wind could have carried her off. Even planning to be together was no guarantee. If she didn't show, he'd remind her of the plans they'd made and she'd say, 'That was your plan.' So he stopped planning. And she stopped being expected, so she could never be late or be a no-show. For a while, it was a mutually agreeable arrangement. Dad said she considered me one of his plans too. Another plan she never agreed to. 'You did this to me,' was a favorite refrain during her pregnancy. I was something that had happened to her. Things that happened could be corrected after the fact. Undone, as it were. Dad told me my mother did say to him once that she thought I was a pretty cool accident as accidents go. I was about ten at the time. She never said it to me. She never directly told me much of anything that I can remember, except for the manic stuff at the end. The shit I really shouldn't have taken to heart because she didn't know what she was saying or who she was saying it to. But I couldn't help being haunted. It was her eyes. Her wild, dull, probing eyes. I'd go to visit her in the dementia ward. Those eyes fixed on me as she scolded, 'Why did you do this to me'? Or bellowed, 'Mother, just leave me alone!' Or threatened, 'He's mine. You can't have him, bitch.' There are heartwarming stories of people becoming charming and childlike as their brains start shutting down areas where more complex ideas are formed, areas that make us who we are, areas where there's metaphor, subtlety, a creative dissonance, and memories that retain a sense of time and place. My mother wasn't charming or childlike. Maybe it was because the two of us never did take to each other. My dad said I didn't latch on well as a newborn, and the nursing, when she would nurse, was no relief to her. A leech at her breast wasn't a bonding moment; it was just an extension of the inconvenience of the pregnancy. She had me and she considered that the beginning and end of the contract we had entered into. A bottle replaced the breast after a couple of weeks and, more often than not, according to Dad, he was left holding the bottle. I imagine my relationship with my mother was similar to a military kid's experience. She'd go away, the way soldiers and sailors go away, and then she'd show up again for a while. She might even bring a gift, like the model of the Jaguar XK-E convertible that's still displayed on my dresser. When she gave it to me, I was seventeen and asked what it was. She said, 'It's beautiful.' We bonded briefly over late-night ice cream and stories of adventures in places like Taos or the Yucatan or Belize. And then one morning Dad was sitting up alone watching the sunrise through the steam of his coffee. I asked where my mother was and he told me she had to leave again. 'She'll be back,' he assured me, then tapped the chair next to him and invited me to admire the mix of pink and lavender on the horizon. My father's heart may have been as fickle as my mother's head, but he never left me. Not once. Or just the one time. The last time.*

"Sorry," June says, "what was that? I couldn't hear you."

"Conspicuous absence," Rose says, louder this time. "That about sums her up. Did you bring cookies?"

# WARRIOR HAWKS

*Monday, May 11*

Kelsey fixes Rose her breakfast and takes it to her roost on the balcony. Rain is forecast, but the morning clouds are thin, and the air is still. Looking next door, he sees that the boys left weekend work unfinished. Boards for a raised-bed garden are laid out in June's backyard. A shame to leave such a simple task undone for another week.

"June's crew didn't finish up yesterday," Kelsey explains to Rose. "I'm going to offer to help her out this morning."

"It's June now, is it?" Rose says.

Kelsey hears a cautionary note in her tone. She must want him to know this is not a rhetorical question. He smiles and delicately draws his index finger across her raised eyebrows.

"Oh my, is that jealousy I see creeping across your supercilium? That's a good sign. There's some spunk in the old girl yet."

Her brow doesn't relax under his touch. "And what about the old fart? Is he feeling spunky?"

Kelsey steps back. "Now you're being silly. Assembling a raised bed out of two-by-eights will take no time at all. I'll be back before you even miss me."

"Don't make—a pest of yourself. I don't want you—scaring her off."

"June will not be shy about telling me if I'm being a pest. And besides, this is just one thing. It isn't as if she has a to-do list."

"Not yet," Rose counters, through an exaggerated pout.

"Stop that. Here's your bell. I'm just a ring away."

"Yes, you are," she says. The words are sharp, distinct. Kelsey takes their sting in stride. Jealousy, he is becoming ever more certain, is a natural impulse of the survival instinct. She is blameless. She can't help it. It makes perfect sense.

The work of connecting four boards that have been precut to prescribed lengths is, as Kelsey predicted, almost mindlessly simple. After reviewing the job and making sure they have all the necessary tools and materials, he begins drilling.

June stops him with a hand on his shoulder. "Kelsey, you'll want to drill on the side, not the top."

He hesitates for a moment to process her correction. "Of course," he says, and flips the board.

He hesitates again. June says, "Here, let me mark the board so you don't have to eyeball it." She makes two pencil marks about an inch from the end of the board. "There you go. Straight through now."

He picks up on her teacherly tone. She may talk to the boys this way, but he is not one of them. His face tightens around the eyes and mouth. "I'm quite capable," he reminds her.

"I'm sorry," June says. "Old habits."

Kelsey forgives her and returns to his task. They continue in silence and construct two corners before June says, "You have an anniversary coming up next month, right?"

The personal nature of the question takes Kelsey by surprise. He stops drilling and replies with a cheery, "Yes, we do. Marking forty-seven terrifying years."

June recoils. "Terrifying? That's not very nice."

Kelsey is disappointed his humor has missed the mark. "I'm sorry. I didn't mean it as it must have sounded. It's not the years themselves that were terrifying. That they have passed is what's terrifying. And that we won't make forty-eight."

June seems dismayed by his response. "I suppose that's one way to look at it." The way she says it suggests to Kelsey she thinks it is precisely the wrong way to look at it.

He lines up and drills another pilot hole, then says, "I'm not sure there's another way to view the rolling out of life's ball of string. It's an unrelenting process of diminution, is it not? Rose is teaching us that, don't you think?"

June rearranges the screws she's holding so that they're all facing the same way. "No, I don't think that." She gives Kelsey a look that he sees as genuine concern, as if maybe she feels sorry for him. It is the most delicate contradiction Kelsey has ever experienced.

"Of course you don't," he says. "Your eyes are still reliable; your joints don't yet talk back."

June is not amused. "You may not believe it, but my knees do complain. Despite that, I still think there are little wonders revealed with age. Things we could never know when we were younger."

Kelsey sets one buttock on a two-by-eight and rests the drill on his thigh. "These little wonders…" His response is interrupted by a brilliant golden glow that first burns out June's face and then expands to form a circle around her head. It is a blazing aura, like the Sun God on his chariot, like the Madonna incarnate. He looks down and closes his eyes.

June puts her hand on his shoulder. "Are you okay?"

Kelsey cautiously raises his head and opens his eyes. June has returned to her earthly incarnation. "Yes," he says. He considers sharing his vision but is reminded of something Rose said. *How much decrepitude can June stand?* Instead he says, "Just a little lightheaded."

"Are you sure you're okay? Did you feel any pain? Do you need some water?"

"No, no pain. No water, thank you. Just remind me what we were taking about."

June looks Kelsey over as if holding back her answer until she is sure he's not going to pass out on her. "We were talking about growing old," she says.

"Yes," he responds brightly. "And you spoke of little wonders, am I right?"

"That's right," June says, with what Kelsey reads as relief.

"These wonders, as you call them, don't result in a rolling out of more time. One moment we notice something that has likely been presented to us a thousand times before with little or no notice on our part. Say, for example, the way the moon looks at a particular time of year, or the subtle colors of a female cardinal, or the scent of cinnamon. We thrill at our noticing, assign it some grand significance, and then off we go to the next moment, our little wonder rapidly receding into the neuronal netherworld where memories go to die, only to be reconstructed as something new in some future moment."

June cocks her head at him and says, "That's a very odd perspective coming from a man who's spent his life fascinated by the tiniest details of nature."

Kelsey concedes her point with a shrug.

"But I'm not talking about those things," June says. "I'm thinking of what we learn about ourselves. You and Rose are very lucky to have had a long life together. I see that as something that makes you more, not less. I try to think of what I receive from each day, not what it takes away. Memories are memories. Today is today."

"Okay," Kelsey says, not entirely sure he understands. "But nature is rather clear on this point. Whatever you think of the moments that came before today, you have fewer moments left. That's the terrifying bit, right?"

June watches as a squirrel that has somehow lost half its tail hangs upside down from her bird feeder pilfering sunflower seeds. Rather than upsetting her, Kelsey senses her admiration of the handicapped bandit's acrobatic assault.

"Maybe," she says in the squirrel's direction, "they were never your moments." She turns back to Kelsey and adds, "Maybe only the terror is yours."

"The terror?" he says.

"It sounds to me like you're afraid of what will happen after Rose dies. It's your fear that's making all those past moments so terrifying."

Her directness puzzles Kelsey. He isn't clear how they got here. He feels as if he's walked into someone else's conversation. He asks, "Have you been talking to Rose about me?"

"No, of course not. It's just that listening to you makes me think maybe this is why you…I don't know…forgive me if I get this wrong…but you try so hard to pretend everything is okay, that you're okay. I know what it's like to lose someone you love dearly. I know the loneliness, the sadness. I know how fragile you can feel and, at the same time, how hard it can be to admit you could use a little help working through it all. I'm sorry. I don't mean to project my own experience on you. I hope I haven't upset you."

Kelsey shifts his seat and repositions the drill in his lap. He cannot bring himself to meet June's eyes. He had assumed June's caretaking was reserved for Rose. He never dared imagine she might have the caring capacity for two. He can think of nothing to say. They sit like this—June rearranging the screws in the palm of her hand, Kelsey watching the breeze rustle the lilac bush—for several befuddled seconds before the silence is broken by three clearly distinguished *dings* from across the driveway. Kelsey is relieved to have been summoned.

"Esmeralda calls," he says. "I'll come back to help finish this up."

"No rush. I'll be here."

⤶

When Kel steps out on the deck, Rose admits, "I cheated with three bells. Wasn't sure you'd hear me—over your talking, drilling. Really isn't urgent. Hope you don't mind."

"Of course not," Kel says. "How may I be of service?"

Rose decides to ignore his tone of disguised annoyance.

"I'd like to shift over—to the recliner."

They manage the transfer easily enough. Rose feels more in her body than she has in some time. She asks Kel to bring out her floppy hat, cashmere shawl, and the top book from her bedside table. As she arranges the shawl over her shoulders, Kelsey asks why she really called him home.

"I'm curious what you—think of June. Do you find her interesting? Clever? Pretty?"

Kel is stood up by the question, as if he finds it somehow provocative. Rose takes this as confirmation that his fondness for June comes with a pang of guilt, suggesting a more than neighborly attraction. She watches his face work through the futility of either feigning innocence or posturing denial. He surprises her with feisty nonchalance.

"All three, I suppose, but in reverse order." He retreats to the bedroom to get the tray he used to carry up her lunch.

"So, is it a timeline—or rank order?"

Kel returns with the tray and starts loading dishes. "You hardly touched this," he says.

"Don't change the subject."

"Please repeat the question."

"Are you saying you found her—pretty before you found her—interesting, or that you find her prettier—than she is interesting?"

"Ah, the former," he replies, seeming now to be enjoying the exchange. "That she is attractive is self-evident. Talking to her I've learned that she is interesting, though not always in a good way. She can be a bit naïve and churchy, which aren't very appealing characteristics in a mature woman. It suggests she's been underexposed."

Rose can't help feeling a bit wounded by the pleasure Kel is taking in rising to her bait. "Any descriptors I've missed?" she asks, hoping he will hear it as facetious.

Kel takes advantage. "Several. Kind, generous, patient, friendly, caring, considerate—"

"Stop it!" This is some other Kel, salting the wound. Since receiving her death sentence, she's been spoiled by doting Kel. Doting Kel would've called her self-pity bluff and countered with hyperbolic flattery. This is not doting Kel.

"You asked," he says flatly.

"How then would you—describe me?"

"What are you doing, Rose? Do we have a problem?"

She's unprepared for his turning the tables. She tries to firm her face, but she can feel it droop under the weight of her regret. She drops her chin so that her hat brim gives her cover.

"You don't," she says. "I do. I'm not ready to—give you up yet."

"Give me up?" He stops loading the tray. "What am I

missing? Have you received a trade-in offer I'm unaware of? Is my lease up?"

"Don't be coy. You don't do coy well."

"So, this really is about June?"

Rose doesn't respond.

Kel pulls up a chair and leans forward so he can see under her hat brim. "I had no idea you would be girlish enough to see our neighbor as a threat. I guess I should be flattered that you don't see me as so broken-down that a woman as lovely as Mrs. Danhill would be interested."

"June," Rose snaps.

"Yes," Kel says, and bursts into spontaneous recital. "June from the Roman Juno. Daughter of Saturn. Mother of Mars. Protector of women. Goddess of love and marriage and—" He cuts himself off and returns to the lunch tray.

"Oh, don't stop," she wheezes. "You were saying?"

"And the sixth month of the Gregorian calendar," he says.

"You coward. You gleefully ran—right up to that cliff. Say it, Kel. Goddess of love—and marriage—and what?"

"Let's stop, Rose. We don't want to do this."

"But I think we do. I think we must."

Kel sinks to a knee beside her. "To what end, my sweet?"

"Don't you dare. That won't defuse your—smoking petard."

He looks at her with such wretchedness that she is instantly sorry she has lit this fuse. He stands, turns from her, and leans on the balcony railing. *How he must hate me. It's trouble enough that I'm not June, but that I have become this withered, wicked thing is more than he can handle. Can I blame him if he turns from me?*

Kelsey talks over the railing as if addressing an audience but in a voice only she can hear. "I'll finish up this chore and it will be the last. I thought—" He stops himself again. Rose doesn't fill the silence this time. "You invite her over. I thought you liked her. I thought—" He turns from the railing and, without looking at Rose, picks up the tray and walks away with long, purposeful strides.

*Oh, shit. What have I done?*

ᴥ

What remains of the raised-bed assembly takes only minutes. Kelsey drives the last few screws without initiating any conversation. June reciprocates with silence. He helps her position the assembled rectangle and packs up his drill. She asks after Rose and he assures her she is fine. Because he is so short with his responses, June asks again if he is okay. "I didn't cross a line I shouldn't have, did I? I didn't mean to—"

"No, no. Everything's fine," Kelsey says. "I need to get back to my desk is all. Enjoy your new garden."

"Thank you. I hope I didn't upset you earlier."

"Upset me? How?"

June can see he is genuinely bewildered by her comment. "Never mind," she says.

He leaves without responding, clearing the boxwoods in a surprisingly nimble single stride.

June sits on the new flowerbed frame and examines her neighbors' house. A house with too many rooms for two people with too many stairs and too much exterior to maintain. She tries to imagine their forty-seven years. She wonders what the world looks like to people with all those years of shared history. What does the professor see when he looks out his window? Is the terror of all the passing moments inside those walls or out here? To June, the inside of their house feels like a sort of sanctuary, not the prison the professor hints at. It's familiar, personal. On the outside everything is always changing. She knows the terror in that, in the uncertainty, the indifference of the world. She could understand if he pulled his curtains and tried to suspend time, to cling to those fleeting moments that he says get lost in memory. But he keeps the curtains open. He must find some solace in all the hubbub of spring. It can't all be terrible. June thinks of the comfort she takes in just about any distraction from the inevitability of her own life. She knows Rose feels the same. There must be something that comforts the professor.

ᴥ

He's back at his desk. He understands now—with sudden, diamond-like clarity—what a distraction June has become. Weeks ago, he was sure he was on to something. The epigenetic angle had promise. He was confident it was something the *New Yorker* or *Atlantic* or *Nature* would consider. A daring, speculative piece by a distinguished bug scholar. And his colleagues would be intrigued, forced to delve deeper into the biomechanics of the hypothesis. And yet, he set it aside. He was so easily taken in by June's world. Seduced by the easy sway of her movements. Her resplendent flesh. The full flush and proximity of her life.

*I'll pull the curtains. Silence the air. Focus on my work, my words.*

### 3 | THE PSYCHOPATHY GAMBIT

*The theory that an organism's experience—particularly of trauma— leads to patterns of behavior that can imprint on the offspring of the organism and affect the expression of the offspring's genes has received sufficiently broad acceptance; however, that such behavior can include widespread sexual deceit and sexual cannibalism is something that demands greater attention. These behaviors undermine fundamental precepts of intraspecies communication and the survival of subgroups within the species. There are implications here for* H. sapiens.

*Kent Bailey, professor emeritus in clinical psychology at Virginia Commonwealth University advanced the theory that violent competition within and between proximal ancestral groups was the primary evolutionary precursor of psychopathy. An individual's ability to seek and kill prey and aggressive neighbors, Bailey argues, benefits the tribe. He refers to these individuals as "warrior hawks." Those ruthlessly adept at these skills would be valued and also have a reproductive advantage, both because of the attractiveness of their lethal proclivities to a potential mate and because of the warrior hawk's willingness to resort to lethal means to maintain its place in the tribe. However, such cutthroat warriors present a problem during times of peace and plenty. They can, as has been observed in the historical record of the ferocious Norse warriors, turn against members of their own community.*

Kelsey takes a break to help Rose when a light rain arrives and she asks to return to bed for a late-afternoon nap.

His second break is to prepare dinner. His frame of mind has been buoyed by the day's writing. He looks forward to enjoying the evening meal with Rose. He enters the dining room with his tray and is lucky not to drop the entire display when he discovers Rose sitting at the dining table.

"Hi," she says.

Kelsey steadies himself and the dinner tray. "Oh, hello. You're here. I didn't hear the lift."

"Sorry." A broad, ghoulish smile stretches her lips to the limits of their elasticity. "I descended under cover of—Barber's adagio. Didn't mean to—sneak up on you."

"Well…" Kelsey shifts uncomfortably, trying to figure out the appropriate next move. "Welcome to Café K." He sets the tray on the table. "We are delighted to have you. Excuse me while I spruce up."

The latest bouquet June placed on the table has begun to wilt. He whisks it off to the kitchen and returns with a rag to wipe the table. After he removes the dull film, Rose flinches from the image she casts in the reflective surface. Kelsey is quick to add placemats to the table setting. Candles make up for not having fresh flowers.

He is in good spirits despite the morning's unpleasantness and his mood cheers Rose as well. They linger over their meal and its afterglow. When they cap the evening with a black truffle amaro—a treat they haven't indulged in for months—the morning's animosity is officially washed away. He's convinced his work is the key. Pulling the curtains and blocking out the distraction restored an equilibrium he had upset these last few weeks. *I will miss the birds. But it's a small price to pay.*

"Kel?" Rose says, and fingers her cordial glass.

"Yes, *gioia mia?*"

"I'd like to have June—over for dinner."

# THE INVITATION

June is sitting on her porch swing anticipating the nine o'clock church bells, the hour she has arranged to be picked up by her birding buddies. She is reviewing her life list, noting how many birds she still needs to check off that many other club members have already spotted. The hooded merganser and broad-winged hawk. *How could I have missed them?* she wonders. Even half-blind Kelly Lane has spotted the eastern kingbird that has so far eluded June. Cyril, the club president who is due to pick her up any minute, often boasts of his two sightings of the rare horned lark. Some claim one of those sightings was aural and shouldn't count, but Cyril insists he has visually confirmed both. No one is really in a position to argue with him. Cyril, a man whose squat body, round dark eyes, and unruly white eyebrows give him the look of a screech owl, has been identifying birds for nearly forty years on expeditions to five continents, some of which he has led and lectured on. One birdsong season Cyril and his partner Evan spent two months driving an RV across the continent so Cyril could chronicle the morning bird songs along the way. Evan isn't a birder, but he went along as Cyril's scribe and chef. He was rewarded with a lovely dedication in Cyril's *Morning Song: Waking with the Birds of North America.* June considers Cyril's experience fascinating and his arrogance well-earned. He can stand in a field with his eyes closed and identify the voices of a dozen birds as if they were personal friends speaking directly to him before June can sort out the adolescent yellow warbler from the goldfinch.

Despite her limited skills, she doesn't want to cheat her list. If she can't make out the camouflaged female winter wren that everyone swears is on the second branch from the top of the pine tree just across the marsh, she won't tick it off. Once Cyril offered his Zeiss binoculars to help her locate a distant male indigo bunting. As soon as she raised his ridiculously expensive field glasses to her eyes, the bird popped into view the way the eye chart sharpens when her optometrist dials in her lens prescription. She can't afford such luxurious assistance. She focuses on enjoying the chase and tries to avoid having her pleasure depend on a particular outcome. Cyril calls her a pure birder. She thinks it's his nice way of saying inept.

The club is headed to the wildlife refuge at Tinicum, a favorite habitat for migrating birds. It's peak spring migration time. The day is mild and clear. Going midweek will mean fewer people. June is confident it will be a fruitful quest.

The bell tower strikes up its four-bar chorus leading into the hour's nine chimes. Cyril's Land Rover is not yet in sight. June hears a bustling behind her and turns. The professor is making his way through the bushes and across her driveway.

"Good morning," he says.

"Good morning, Professor."

His approach, she observes, is uncharacteristically subdued. He doesn't even protest her addressing him as professor. The gloom of yesterday afternoon seems to have carried over to this morning.

"I saw you sitting. I hope you don't mind the intrusion."

"Not at all. What's up?"

"Binoculars and a utility vest," Kelsey says. "Not typical attire for porch sitting."

"I'm going birding with my club," she says.

"Birding?" His voice lifts, signaling a sudden shift in attitude. "How do I not know about this?"

June shrugs.

"You know, I have just this year come to notice how many different species live right here." Kelsey speaks with what June sees as exaggerated enthusiasm. "It's quite amusing. I'm thinking of taking up bird-watching as a hobby."

"Really?" June says, hoping she doesn't sound too skeptical.

"All your visits and this has never come up. I can't believe I have an expert living next door."

"Hardly an expert. But the club is fun."

"What do you call yourselves?"

"Bluestone Birders."

"Wonderful." He nods then pauses. June senses him again switching internal gears. His sobriety restored, Kelsey says, "Rose really enjoys your visits."

June is a little confused by this unremarkable news; she has been coming by almost daily now for several weeks. "That's nice to know. I enjoy them too."

"She's wondering if you'd like to come over for dinner?"

Dinner with the Geddeses. Rose and the professor in the same room for an entire meal. June finds the thought a bit over-whelming. But since he's speaking hypothetically, she blurts out, "Sure. That'd be great."

As if on cue, Cyril pulls up to the end of the driveway. June stands. She hesitates so it doesn't seem like she's rudely running off. "Here's my ride. Thanks for thinking of me. Let me know when—"

"How about one week from today? Around six-thirty?"

"A week?" she repeats, trying to call up a mental calendar.

"Tuesday the nineteenth, I believe," Kelsey clarifies.

The date has no built-in excuse and June can't think of an artificial one that won't sound phony. "Possibly," she says as she begins to walk backwards down the driveway.

"Tuesday then," Kelsey presses.

"I guess," she says. Then quickly adds, "May I bring some-one?"

"The more, the more-ier," the professor says, and smiles broadly. "See you then."

June turns and walks briskly to the car. She settles into the front passenger seat. She glances over her shoulder as they pull away and sees the professor smiling and waving from her driveway.

On the drive to Tinicum, June confesses to Cyril her mixed

feelings about accepting a formal social invitation from her neighbors. "Rose is a very interesting person. But there's a desperation—no, that's an unfair choice of words. There's fear or anger…something that makes me feel I have to choose every word so carefully. While I'm tiptoeing through our conversations, Rose is almost confessional in a just-between-us-girls sort of way, as if we're old friends. I like her a lot. But I'm not sure I'm up to an entire dinner of what she considers casual conversation. And then there's the professor. Up until yesterday, he was like a puppy dog eager to be friends. Then, after helping me put together a raised bed, he suddenly turned cold and distant and I thought it was the last I would ever see of him. Now here he is back again talking about becoming a birder and inviting me to dinner as if nothing happened. Sometimes it's all a bit much."

"If you need a winggirl," Cyril says, "I'm your man. Evan's away early next week. Meeting your crazy neighbors sounds much more exciting than kung pao chicken and *The Walking Dead*."

June gratefully accepts his offer.

# THE ARRANGEMENT

### *Saturday, May 16*

Kelsey is raking out the front gardens when a boy he recognizes but whose name escapes him makes a showy arrival next door. The boy is wearing red headphones and swaying his hips side to side like he's dancing with his bicycle, a bike so small he has to pedal standing up. He extends his right arm at shoulder level and pulses it up and down to the private beat of his music. He pedals up the driveway to join the two other boys already at work cutting up tree branches the recent storm winds brought down in June's yard. Kelsey rakes his way toward the edge of the yard to watch the goings on.

The handsaw the tall boy is using to cut the branches seems to be working him more than he is working it. Without coming to a full stop, the late arrival steps away from the bike, lets it rattle to the ground, and pulls down his headphones so they drape around his neck.

"Wussup, my Js?" he bellows.

"Nice bike," the sawing boy mutters. "Where'd you steal that?"

"Relax. Borrowed, not stolen. It'll be home before it's missed."

The tall boy tightens his grip on the saw handle. "What are you doing here?" He seems to be challenging the late arrival, but his demeanor has little effect. Late arrival walks right up to him.

"Came to see what you hardworking young men are up to. Thought maybe you could use a hand."

"We don't have that much to do today. We can handle it."

"That's good, cuz I need Little. I came to scoop him."

"What for?" the tall boy asks.

"That's not your business. It's my business and I need Little."

June is in her vegetable garden about thirty feet away. She stands up and calls out, "Is everything all right?"

"Yes, ma'am," the tall boy answers, then lowers his voice and says to late arrival, "Little's helping me right now. You can talk to him when we're done."

Late arrival surveys the scene. "What're you doing?"

"What does it look like?"

"Let me see that saw."

The tall boy pulls the saw out of the branch and steps back. "We can do it. We don't need your help."

Late arrival moves close enough to take the saw if the tall boy won't give it up. "Just give me the saw," he says, sounding very much in charge. "You can keep the money. Means shit to me."

The tall boy drops the saw and walks away. Late arrival picks it up and goes after the branch like it insulted him. Each of his strokes does twice the damage of the tall boy's. He's finished with the first section and on to the second within a minute. The youngest of the three picks up the cut segment and places it in the garbage can so gently he doesn't attract any attention from the other two. The tall boy starts clipping the suckers off a second branch. Late arrival takes a quick break to flex and shake out his hand, then resumes his assault. Kelsey is impressed with how quickly he has dispatched the first branch.

Tall boy carries the second branch to the cutting area. "I can do this one," he says.

Late arrival flips the saw and holds it out handle first. "Let me know when you're tired."

Tall boy struggles through the first section. The branch needs three more cuts, each section thicker than the one before. He shakes out his hand and lines up the saw to start the second cut.

Late arrival sits in the driveway leaning back on straight arms, his shoulders hunched around his ears, and talks to no one in particular.

"The day is slipping away. It's a big old world of missed

opportunity out there. And all for what? Some chump change, ballbusting work. So much having to be had and I'm here waiting on you like some loser have not. You've got a minute to get through this next cut, then Superman's coming to the rescue."

Halfway through the branch the saw snags and tall boy's wrist buckles. He releases the saw as if it bit him and turns away shaking out his hand and cussing under his breath.

Late arrival is up and over the branch before tall boy turns back around. He braces the branch on his knee to widen the cut and free up the blade. He finishes the cut in a flurry of strokes. Tall boy sits holding his wrist, pretending the injury is the only reason he isn't trying to get the saw back. Late arrival finishes the last section then holds the saw out to tall boy.

"You okay to cleanup, gimp?"

Tall boy snatches the saw but says nothing. Late arrival calls out to the little one, "Let's go."

Little boy looks at tall boy.

"I said let's go," late arrival repeats, sounding like the boss.

Little boy drops the branch parts he has collected and obeys. Late arrival straddles the bike as little boy climbs onto the handlebars and balances as steady as a hood ornament.

Watching late arrival dissever the branches so impresses Kelsey, he hails him as the overburdened bicycle starts down the driveway. Late arrival drops his feet, just managing to keep his friend balanced in front of him.

"What?" the boy snaps.

"I'm wondering if I can talk you into coming over tomorrow to do some work," Kelsey says.

"Me?"

"Yes. Just you." Kelsey turns to the hood ornament and says, "No offense, young man, but this is a two-person job."

Hood ornament shifts his butt on the handlebars.

"Yardwork really isn't my thing," late arrival says. "You should talk to TJ."

"I've watched the three of you. I like the way you handled that saw. I think you're the right man for the job if you want it."

Late arrival examines the professor as if looking for an

indication that this is some sort of a trick. But Kelsey is all business and the boy can tell. The boy smiles. "What are you paying?"

Kelsey smiles back. "Well, that's a topic for tomorrow's discussion."

"As long as you don't use that poor, retired professor line, we might have something to talk about."

"Well, I am a retired professor, but not poor. Come talk to me. How's noon?"

"Make it one. I need my beauty rest."

"One o'clock it is. Oh, and be careful. That doesn't look very safe."

"What, this? This is a natural bicycle built for two. Right, Little?"

"Right," hood ornament echoes under his breath.

"Tomorrow then," Kelsey says.

The boy runs the bike back into motion and jumps up on the pedals. Kelsey tenses as rider, hood ornament, and bike swerve wildly left then right. The boy regains control and runs the stop sign at the main road. His bravado makes Kelsey cringe and smile. He tries on the boy's square-shouldered, swaying walk back to check on Rose. It looks so loose and effortless on the boy, but it's hard to keep it up all the way to the house.

&#8766;

June stands up to check on the boys' progress just as Big rides off with Joey perched precariously on his handlebars. TJ is picking up pieces of branches.

"Is Joey okay, TJ?" she calls out. "He didn't cut himself, did he?"

"No, ma'am, he's fine." TJ slams the last section of tree branch into the garbage can.

"How about you? You okay?"

"Yeah." He snatches up the push broom and goes after the saw dust like he's trying to grind it into the asphalt. Even from the distance of the vegetable garden, it's clear this isn't the usually sweet TJ. June removes her gardening gloves, sets them

down beside her trowel, and goes to him. He seems to sense
her coming and pushes the sawdust faster and farther down the
driveway.

"Are you going to sweep that all the way back to Memorial
Park?"

He doesn't answer.

"What's the matter, TJ?"

He continues sweeping away from her. "I'm tired of babysitting."

"Babysitting?"

"Everybody knows he's slow, can't be on his own. Why do I
have to watch out for him? I'm tired of it."

"Maybe you should look at it differently. Look at what it
says about you. Your mother trusts you. You should be proud
of that."

TJ looks at her as if she hasn't the least clue what she's
talking about.

"Then I'm sick of being trusted," he says. "Let somebody
else watch him. What am I supposed to do? Just drop what I'm
doing and follow along because Joe wants Little for something?
Let Joe look out for him if he wants him so bad."

He hammers at the sawdust again for emphasis. June thinks
he's testing an argument he figures he's going to have with his
mother when he goes home. "Where did Big take Joey?" she
asks.

"I don't know. I don't want to know."

"You're worried about him, aren't you?"

He stops and leans wearily on the broom. His voice is that
of an exasperated parent. "Whatever Big's doing, it can't be
good."

"Do you need to go?"

TJ doesn't answer, but looks at her like he's waiting for her
to give him permission.

She grips the broom handle and he lets her take it. "I can
finish up here," June says. "I'll get your money. I'll give you
Joey's too."

"He didn't really do anything today," TJ says. "You can just pay me."

"Are you sure? He was here for most of the hard part."

"I'm sure."

~

When Kelsey returns to the front yard to finish up, he notices June sweeping her driveway. The tall boy doesn't seem to be around. His first thought is to offer assistance. He reminds himself he's supposed to be blocking out the distraction of his neighbor. That he has to keep his focus on his own business, on Rose, on his writing. He knows this, and yet, after a mere moment's hesitation, he crosses the border.

"You seem to have lost your crew," he says. "Need a hand?"

"It's just a little sawdust. I'm all but done."

He watches her work, admiring the economy and efficiency of her movements. All her parts still work with an ease and harmony he envies.

"I've been thinking of giving your boys more work, if it's okay with you, of course."

"They're not exactly *my* boys, Professor."

The admonishment stings a bit, but Kelsey chooses to ignore it. There's a sullen impatience about her attitude he doesn't want to test. He picks up her dustpan and positions it in front of her broom.

"I think they appreciated the convenience of being able to pick up a few extra bucks last time," he says.

June stops sweeping. "As long as the price is fair." She glares down at him with a reproving expression he finds a bit patronizing. It's not the response he expected. He anticipated at least a dash of gratitude for his interest in the young men she seems highly invested in. After all, anything he contributes relieves her of the burden of being their sole benefactor. Certainly, she can see this is a good thing.

"Of course," Kelsey says. "I'll pay their rate. In fact, I've hired one of them to help me build a compost pit."

"TJ?" June asks.

"I'm not sure about names," Kelsey admits. "The sturdier, louche fellow. He seems very industrious."

"Big Joe?" Her voice registers concern.

"That sounds right. He's coming tomorrow. Is there a problem?"

"Interesting," June says, and resumes pushing dust into the pan Kelsey is repositioning for her. "I've always found Big to be the most reluctant of them. Maybe he'll respond better to you."

"Perhaps," Kelsey says, and smiles. Her return smile is unconvincing. Maybe it's the angle, looking up at her from this kneeling position. She seems to have put herself on the boys' side of the proposed arrangement rather than seeing him as partnering with her. He can't quite put his finger on what it is about the manner in which he's communicating that is failing to elicit reciprocity. It must be clear to her his intentions are honorable. He sighs audibly.

"Thank you," June says, ignoring his frustration.

"Of course." Kelsey tips the dustpan into the garbage. The sawdust sparkles as it falls. Like flakes of gold catching the morning sun. A glittering gold cataract. The effect is almost blinding. "How beautiful."

"Excuse me?" June says.

"The sawdust. The way it burst into a shower of gold."

"Sounds lovely." Her tone is skeptical. "Sorry I missed it."

"Me too. It was quite astonishing."

June studies him for a moment and asks, "While you're here, would you mind helping me carry the cans to the curb?"

The cans are easily managed by the two of them. Kelsey doesn't let on that the first trip put a bit of a strain on his left wrist. He makes a point of reversing their positions on the second can so he uses his right hand. The nonchalance with which she handles her half of the effort suggests that she could have dragged the cans to the curb herself. Her asking him to help is encouraging, a nod to their evolving friendship. Given the sour note the visit started on, he's quite pleased with how it has progressed. At the curb he says, "So, we'll see you Tuesday for dinner. Will you be bringing someone?"

"Oh yes. I should have told you. My friend Cyril. He picked me up the other day."

"The birder?"

"Exactly. He's looking forward to meeting you."

It's Kelsey's turn to be skeptical, but he says nothing; he simply nods and excuses himself.

From the balcony, Rose can see Kel come through the back gate. She's been listening to the comings and goings in her neighbor's driveway and is eager to hear about what she has missed.

"What's going on next door?" she calls down.

"What was that, dear?"

"Next door. What's going on?"

"I'll be right up, *principessa.* I can't hear you."

Kel goes into the house and then quickly out again. He goes out the gate and heads back up the driveway. A moment later he's back, this time with the rake. He returns it to the garden shed and comes back to the house. She hears water running in the kitchen. After a few minutes, the radio comes on. He's still in the kitchen.

*The son of a bitch has forgotten me.*

# A Task at Hand

*Sunday, May 17*

There's a knock at the back door, first on the door frame and then, before Kelsey can answer, a second sharper rapping on one of the glass panels. A familiar yet maddeningly nameless young man is standing on the back porch. Kelsey opens the door enough to step outside and pulls it closed behind him.

"Can I help you?"

The boy says, "Thought I was supposed to be the one helping you, Professor."

"Yes, yes, of course. But aren't you early?"

"Yeah, well, time is money, right? Early bird eats the worm and all that."

"Indeed. However, I was just heading to the hardware store to pick up a few things I need for the job. It's not far. Would you like to come along?"

"Nah, I'll wait here. Save my strength for your mystery project."

"Okay." Kelsey gathers himself. He pats his pockets to confirm he has his wallet. His keys and a list are in his hand. "Can I get you anything before I go? We have lemonade if I'm not mistaken."

"No, sir, I'm good. You go ahead." He sits down on the porch step and leans back on his elbows. "I'll just sit here and be right on time when you get back."

"I'll make this quick," Kelsey says. "It's not far." He starts down the steps, stops halfway, and asks, "Remind me of your name."

"Joe. Or Big. Either one."

"Right. Thank you. I'll be right back, Joe."

☙

"Whhhhaaat? Man, this is some crazy shit!"

The voice is coming from the hallway outside of Kel's office. Rose heard Kel leave, so who's in the house? It's a voice she's never heard before. A man. And Kel isn't responding to it. The voice is carrying on a private conversation. Rose's heart registers that she is eavesdropping on an intruder. She tries to calm it with slow breaths.

"Lantern Fly," the voice announces. "I'd hate to step into any pile of shit you've been buzzing around. Oh man, there is no way that scorpion is real. Professor, you're into some serious beasts. These better not be Marrsville beasts."

He's quiet now but moving. His steps creak in the hall. He's outside her door. No. He's in the room. She can feel his presence even before she sees him emerge from the small bedroom antechamber. A young man with short red hair and thin sideburns the length of his ears. He doesn't see her yet. His eyes are fixed on her jewelry box on the dresser. Suddenly he senses something and hunches defensively. His knees flex. He swivels to his left and the two of them lock eyes. He brings his clenched fist to his mouth.

"Oh, shit." He winces and then straightens to take a hard look at the body in the bed. "Ooh, lady, I'm sorry. I didn't know. Damn. Excuse me. Ah, man, you're like the Crypt Mistress."

Rose draws in as much life as possible, swells herself into something resembling a physical presence, and speaks as reproachfully as she can muster. "Who are *you*?"

"It's all right." He waves his hands dismissively. "I'm just waiting on the professor."

"What are you—doing here?"

"He asked me. Hey, I can't catch what've got, can I?"

"You shouldn't be *here*," she says. But the scolding she assumes she's projecting is lost on the boy. He sits down on the edge of Kel's bed.

"The professor went for supplies," he says. "So, I thought I'd have a look around. Didn't know you were here. Really."

"You shouldn't—be *here*."

"Don't worry. I won't bite. There's not much of you to bite anyway."

Rose picks up her cell phone, but before she can even activate the phone function, the boy takes it from her and sets in down on Kel's nightstand.

"There's no need for that."

Rose pounds on her bell. The boy covers his ears.

"Damn. Stop that. Nobody can hear you."

She keeps pounding, hoping June is in her garden. The boy comes around the bed and grabs the bell.

"Calm down," he says. "I get it. I'll go. I didn't mean anything."

He puts the bell back down. Rose's pill box catches his eye.

"Damn. What've you got in here? Ooh, Mighty Mo. Guess you're one foot in. That can't be fun."

"No, it isn't. You should leave."

"I will. I just want to see that before I go." He walks to the dresser and picks up the model car Rose keeps next to her jewelry box. "Nice. Nineteen-sixty-one Jaguar XK-E. A classic."

"That's mine," Rose says, her voice childishly desperate. "Don't touch."

"Yours?" He gestures with the model as if he's forgotten it's in his hand. "You like cars?"

"That one, yes."

"Why this one?"

"It's beautiful."

"True," he nods. "True that." He replaces the car. "So, if you like beautiful cars, why's the professor driving an old Volvo?"

"Practical."

He nods again and comes back to the foot of the bed. "Hey, what's with all the giant bugs in the other room?"

"He studies them," Rose says.

"That's like a job, studying bugs?"

"Entomology."

"En–to–mol–o–gy," he repeats. "Fancy word. Bugs are just bugs. What's with all these fancy ologies. Like phar–ma–col–o–gy.

It's just drugs, right? Should be bugology and drugology, right?"

She doesn't consider it a serious question. When she offers neither a comment nor a laugh, the boy turns and walks to the open French doors. He steps out on the balcony.

"This is nice. I like this. You sit out here much?" She starts to respond but he doesn't wait. "I'd sit out here all the time if this was my place."

He plops into a chair at the café table and puts his feet up on the opposite chair. He laces his fingers behind his head. She's furious watching him, and jealous. Such audacious youth. There's quiet between them, Rose smoldering on one side of it and the boy luxuriating on the other. They are interrupted by the sound of tires on gravel.

"That's the professor," the boy says. "Time to go work." He steps out of his repose reluctantly. He pauses at the end of the bed and says, "Sorry about whatever's doing this to you."

Rose stares into the hazel eyes of the man-child. There's nothing in them she recognizes at first. None of the sorrow he professes. No coldness either. No pity. And no mocking. The closest she can come to a description of what she sees reflected there is honesty. He is exactly who he is.

"Me too," she says.

Kel has entered the driveway but has stopped before pulling all the way to the back. The boy starts to leave, then pauses again. He senses that he has time. Hesitantly he says, "You know, there're better drugs than that. Stuff that'll make you feel better, I mean." He shrugs and exits with a calculated, panic-free urgency.

As Kelsey pulls into his driveway, he happens on June coming down her porch steps. He lowers his passenger side window and calls out, "Good afternoon. Lovely day."

She takes a couple of steps toward the car. "Yes, it is." Her tone suggests the weather is not of particular interest. He ignores the coolness of her response.

"I hope to make good use of it," he says. "I don't know if

I mentioned that I've hired one of the boys to help me build a compost bin."

"You did mention that just yesterday," June says, and takes another couple of steps toward the car.

"Yes, of course," he says, unable to place exactly when it was they spoke.

"Joe, I believe it is," June says.

"Yes, that's him. Hard worker."

June steps closer and bends toward the window so she can lower her voice. "I've never worked with Joe alone. I hope it goes okay."

"I'm sure it will be fine. He actually showed up early. He's waiting for me. I'd better go."

She stands there hugging herself as he closes the window and pulls up to the end of the driveway.

Kelsey comes through the back gate and finds Joe exactly as he left him, with the exception of the glass of water.

"Hey, Professor," he says, and sips from the glass. "I couldn't find the lemonade."

"No lemonade?" Kelsey says. "We'll have to do something about that later."

He doesn't remember giving the boy permission to go in the house.

"You get your stuff?" Joe asks.

"I did indeed. Please join me at the compost pile."

Joe takes instruction well, works diligently, and is good company, making steady conversation in accompaniment to their steady progress. He asks Kelsey a lot of questions. He wants to know if he's married and, when he's told about Rose he wants to know more about her illness. He asks what Kelsey is a professor of and tells the professor he knows the word entomology. *Clever boy,* Kelsey thinks. Joe wants to know what the biggest bug in the world is. The smallest. And he asks why Kelsey became an entomologist.

"I love the speculation and the anticipation associated with scientific inquiry," Kelsey says, in response to the boy's last question. "The elegance of solid science, of probing the unknown, triangulating the truth by plotting facts, by noticing the tiniest details."

"I don't know what you're talking about, but it sounds pretty. Sounds like church."

Kelsey smiles. "Like church, yes. That's very good. And yet, despite all my passion for the work of the mind, here I am giddy with the simple, predictable reward of our humble task. A task at hand is worth two in the books."

"You just make that up, or is that an old professor joke?"

"Just occurred to me, actually. Do you like it?"

"A little corny."

Kelsey agrees and asks Joe about himself. The boy says there isn't much to tell. "I'm seventeen, well, almost, but people think I'm older because I have my father's build. You know, like a welterweight. And more face hair than most kids my age. Girls think I'm older. That's cool. Problem is, adults expect me to act like them. My aunt. Coaches. Teachers. Guys like you. You're on me all the time about potential and whatever. I didn't ask for this body. I'm just living in it, and I don't think there's much point to making living in it any harder than it has to be."

Kelsey finds it difficult to argue with his adolescent logic. "I agree. Just because someone is physically capable of doing something does not mean he should be compelled to do it. I'm with you on that point."

Joe seems pleased, though Kelsey sees a glint of suspicion in his expression as well. Kelsey can't hold it against the boy. He probably hasn't had many adults come down on his side of an issue over the years.

"What's your father do?" Kelsey asks.

Joe shrugs. "Haven't seen him since I was five."

"Your mother?"

Joe picks up the next board and says, "Can we talk about something else?"

They spend most of the afternoon fencing the compost pile with one-by-fours and chicken wire, then step back to admire their work.

"You know something, young man?" Kelsey says. "I like a

story with a beginning, middle, and end. I'd almost forgotten how much pleasure it gives me to take on a simple task and see it through to its conclusion. After all that cutting and drilling and screwing and running chicken wire, we're left not only with a well-fashioned compost bin, but also with a sense of having accomplished something. Used our hands and minds in service of a thing well done. I hope you feel the same."

"I'm sure I will, Professor, as soon as you pay me."

"You're a practical boy, Joe. I like that."

Kelsey reaches into his pocket for his wallet but all he finds is the receipt from the hardware store. "Well, this is rather inconvenient. I seem to have misplaced my wallet."

"This isn't an old man trick, is it?" Joe asks. "Because I didn't come for the conversation."

"No trick, except on myself, I'm afraid. Let me check my car."

Joe helps Kelsey look under and between the seats and then suggests that they try the hardware store. They drive down together.

Marcy is behind the counter and knows what Kelsey has come for before he asks. "Figured you'd be back, Professor. You left it on the counter. I didn't notice until you'd left. Sorry about that."

"No apology necessary," he says. "I'd leave my head if it weren't screwed on. Unfortunately, it's screwed on a little cockeyed these days." Kelsey waves the reclaimed wallet and says, "Thank you."

He offers Joe a ride to wherever he's going. Joe says he's fine walking.

"Well, then, thanks," Kelsey says. "Your assistance was invaluable."

"Then maybe you'll pay my invaluable rate next time," Joe says.

Kelsey laughs. "I'm not sure what that is. But I imagine it's a bit outside my budget."

Joe notices there's a break in traffic. Taking advantage of the opening, he slaps the roof of Kelsey's car and bounds across the avenue. Once on the other side, he doesn't break stride. He continues like a boxer on a training jog. Kelsey envies him his effortless trot. Watching Joe, Kelsey yearns to be out in the world again, even if like this—without Rose. When he's outside he can sense the life all around him. The squirming in the smoldering warmth of the compost, territorial battles in the trees, insect wings rubbing monotones, the rutting in the woods, young men jogging up the road. What a mean trick it is to sustain sense memory and yearning while daily diminishing one's capacity to satisfy it. Whetting the hunger while wearing down the canines. In a wolf pack, he knows he would be assigned to the pitiable front group, the pacesetting aged and ill who are dependent on others for survival, and are of no use in a hunt or to the she-wolves. But then along come days like today. Some boards, a saw, a drill, some screws, and a scrappy helper. A task at hand. *Maybe June's right. Maybe this can be enough.*

# THE SPIRIT OF ITSELF

*Tuesday, May 19*

When the professor opens the door, he is wearing an apron emblazoned with a yellow triangle within which are the words Man at Work. "Welcome," he says, with a formal sweep of his hand. "You're right on time."

"Sidewalk traffic was surprisingly light for a Tuesday evening," Cyril says, with unfiltered flair.

If they were anywhere but the Geddes's, June would roll her eyes at such an entrance, but in this case, she appreciates Cyril's social ease. She is hoping he will take the evening's spotlight off her.

The professor extends his hand. "Kelsey Geddes."

Cyril's hand casually meets Kelsey's. "Cyril Fugol. Glad to meet you, Professor."

Kelsey gives June an accusatory glare. "She must have taught you that. Kelsey is preferred."

"If I were a professor," Cyril counters, "I would insist that everyone acknowledge it at every opportunity."

Reclaiming his hand Kelsey says, "I see the appellation as something one outgrows. A deciduous adornment."

"To me, being an educator of the highest rank is evergreen," Cyril says. "The grand scope of our ability to know is what separates us from the beasts."

"I think it is rather our growing awareness of all we don't know that is our specific anomaly," Kelsey says.

"If you two are going—to do this all evening—please put me to bed now." Rose's voice, soft but distinct, comes from the living room.

The two men turn toward her. Kelsey says, "My apologies, darling. Cyril, may I present my wife, Rose."

Rose's hair is in a braid only slightly thicker than her finger and is draped over her shoulder. June notes that her understated makeup brings life to a face that a few weeks ago seemed beyond the reach of vanity. Rose's eyes are delicately brightened. The flush in her cheeks is about what a glass of wine might produce. Her lipstick's shade of red is nearly enough to resurrect the full, expressive mouth displayed in the pictures on her bedroom wall.

"*Enchanté*," Cyril offers.

"Aloha," Rose croaks, then pats the spot on the couch next to her and says, "June, push your way past—the insufferables—and come talk to me."

June does as directed and is relieved that the two of them won't start off alone. The men join them for drinks and shrimp cocktail. Cyril and Kelsey's banter turns into something resembling normal conversation. Then, just as June manages to relax, Kelsey announces he needs to check on the roasting potatoes and start the branzino and asparagus. Without checking with June first, Cyril offers to join him, saying he wants to hear more about his praying mantis article.

The men seem to take the lightness that accompanied the small talk with them. June finds it eerie the way the air almost immediately takes on the stagnant weight of Rose's bedroom. Before she can come up with some levity of her own, Rose jumps right in on a favorite topic.

"So, how is he?" she asks.

"Rose, I don't know what you expect me to say…"

"Do you find that—his attention wanders? That his imagination can—be hijacked by the most—farfetched notion—and whisk him away like—a child chasing—a butterfly until—hopelessly lost?"

Her words carry the spirited, damning charge of a detective closing in on the solution to a great mystery. But June sees a silent anguish in Rose's eyes. It's the anguish she decides she needs to appease. "No," June says, "nothing like that. Why are you asking me this?"

"I worry about him. He has been so—forgetful lately. Puts up a good front. I know he's struggling."

The anguish swells. Rose's hands twitch.

"It's normal at his age," June says.

"Not for him," Rose insists. "He was brilliant. Every detail. He prided himself on—details. Now I'm reminding him."

"It must be the stress," June offers, in the hope of guiding Rose away from this discussion.

"You're not hearing me." Rose's eyes are no longer pleading but insisting. "This man—is a fragment—of what he was."

June hesitates. She doesn't want to upset Rose, but she doesn't see all that Rose sees. She knows she can't know all that Rose knows. Agreeing with her, even though only Rose knows the younger man she describes, seems to June as the more fraught path.

"I'm sorry," she says. "I see a man whose mind seems sharp. He's had a couple of dizzy spells while helping me, but I've had my dizzy spells too. And he can be a bit quirky, but that's his charm, right?"

Rose says nothing. June adjusts her position on the couch to a more comfortable distance from her. "Honestly, Rose, I've had few direct dealings with him. I can't say that I would recognize what distraction or decline would look like. Other than the missed squash game and the Post-its perhaps."

"Yes, the Post-its," Rose says.

"I see them as a good thing," June quickly adds. "He wants to be diligent. He doesn't want to fail you. He's got so much to attend to now, and you aren't able to be there next to him all the time. It's a reasonable solution, don't you think?"

Rose shakes her head wearily. "You don't understand."

June presses on. "They're just little household reminders. Probably things you mostly kept track of for him. Like garbage pick-up days and making sure the stove is off."

"No," Rose insists. "It's more. Can't you see? And the boys. You don't find his—interest in the boys odd?"

"Odd? Not really. His interest seems to be in getting work done he doesn't want to take on or needs help with."

"The part that is odd to me," Rose says, "is that he would—have interest now. We've been here over—twenty years. I always pointed out—what needed doing. He never cared if weeds—overtook garden beds—the side of the garage. I struggled to pull him—away from his research—his writing."

June is delighted to be able to interject. "Well, that's a perfect example of something I wouldn't know. I took his interest in the boys at face value. Since caring for you is his first priority, it's only natural he'd want help with yardwork. And I think he knows they appreciate the money."

Rose's wicked smile and slight lowering of her eyes suggests that June's bringing Rose's care into the explanation has had an effect opposite of what June intended. She had hoped reinforcing the professor's commitment to Rose would be reassuring. It seems instead to have struck Rose as more evidence that June is either not paying attention, or that maybe June is keeping something from her.

"Rose, I'm sorry. But I don't know what you want me to say. I don't know what you're not saying. Has something happened I should be aware of?"

The question appears to nudge Rose backwards. She attempts to settle into the couch, but the arrangement of throw pillows causes her to lean awkwardly to one side. June reaches out to reposition the pillows.

Rose doesn't acknowledge the assistance. "No. Nothing happened. Forget I said—anything. I'm just a sick old woman—watching her husband—"

"Dinner is served," Cyril croons and the men emerge from the kitchen laden with platters. Their sudden appearance in the dining room is the cavalry riding to June's rescue. She pops up from the couch and reaches down for Rose's elbow.

"Here, Rose, let me help you."

"Thank you, no. I can manage."

✧

After dinner, reseated in the living room, Kelsey asks his guests to share with him and Rose the story of the bird-watching trip.

June defers to Cyril, who relates the tale of the Tinicum expedition with endearing theatricality. Kelsey is cheered seeing Rose genuinely amused and impressed by Cyril's demonstrations of the various bird calls Rose and Kelsey admit to experiencing as a sort of natural white noise. Cyril imitates the *cheerily, cheer up* and *cheerio* of the robin's daytime carols; the Carolina wren's ringing *tea-kettle tea-kettle tea-kettle* that transitions to *cho-we cho-we cho-we*; the eponymous *chick-a-dee-dee-dee* whose number of *dees*, Cyril explains, signals the size of a threat. "The more *dees*," he reveals, "the smaller and swifter the enemy."

At one point, Kelsey watches with wonder as musical notation pours out of Cyril's mouth and floats about the room, individual notes popping like soap bubbles. He laughs like an enchanted child, which draws amused glances. He doesn't dare attempt to describe the experience. Kelsey takes particular interest when Cyril explains that for the vast majority of species, spring singing is done by males in an attempt to impress the non-singing females. "The females choose their mates," Cyril says, "in large part based on singing prowess as measured by the maturity of tone, muscularity of projection, and the number and complexity of variations on themes. I hope I don't dash any romantic notions of avian fidelity by revealing that paired males continue to sing all spring and summer, and females often spread their tail feathers for Carusos who will have no part in raising their young."

"Fascinating, isn't it," Kelsey says, "how deceitful the natural world can be?"

"He didn't say anything—about deceit," Rose says. "I doubt birdsongs contain—any promise of monogamy—or any other vow."

"Quite right," Cyril says. "There is no promise but for a reproductive tumble in the twigs."

"I stand corrected," Kelsey says, and then shares some of his thoughts on the behaviors he has witnessed outside his window.

When he pauses, June says, "You seem to have spent quite a lot of time watching. I'd say you're already a birder."

"Well, my office is a natural blind," Kelsey says. "All I need to do is look up and there they are on full display."

"So, more voyeur than birder," Cyril says, smiling his self-amusement. "You two should come along on our next outing. We'll teach you proper stalking techniques."

"My walk-in-the-woods days—are over," Rose says.

"How about I come by one morning and we do a little backyard birding?" Cyril offers. "You'd be amazed by what's lurking in the white oaks and your old silver maple."

Kelsey wants to say that if Cyril could see with his eyes, Cyril would be the one amazed by what's living among the ivy and wisteria that cloak the trunk of that old maple. Amazed by the vines themselves, their ability to detach themselves and dance like charmed snakes. Amazed by the faerie creatures that ride the vines. *But this is more than they can know,* he thinks. *More than even they want to know.* So instead he says, "No need for you to make a special trip. I'm sure June can lead a backyard expedition."

"Cyril is so much more skilled than I am," June says. "Honestly, you should take him up on the offer."

There is general agreement to make that happen at everyone's earliest convenience, and then Rose abruptly admits to running out of steam.

"June, could I talk you into—helping me upstairs? Let the men clean."

June assists Rose to her stairlift. Cyril and Kelsey head to the kitchen. Cyril says, "Before dinner, you were talking genetics versus epigenetics…"

✍

June settles Rose onto her pillow and watches her friend's eyes close. Then, as if talking in her sleep, Rose says, "Watch him."

"Yes, of course," June reassures her. "But you shouldn't worry so. It doesn't help Kelsey for you to be fretting. And it certainly doesn't do you any good."

A faint "thank you" is Rose's goodbye.

"I'll see you soon," June says. Rose doesn't respond.

When June turns out the light, for an instant Rose's face glows like a paper lantern lit by a fading candle.

On her way back down the hall, June notices the professor's office door is slightly ajar. Despite all her visits, she has not yet been invited into his room. She nudges the door open another foot. The hinges moan softly. A small desk lamp is on in the otherwise unlit room. The allure of the clutter is irresistible. She can hear the men still chattering away in the kitchen like a couple of jays. She steps through the just-wide-enough opening, taking care not to disturb the piles of magazines, notebooks, and loose papers on the floor. Once clear of the paper barricade, she is overcome by an unmistakable pull of eyes. She is being watched. She does a slow pirouette. Surrounding her on the walls, on the floor leaning against the walls, even propped up in the bookcases, are framed specimens of giant insects. Amazonian insects, carnivorous-looking insects that are frightening even suspended in their displays, frightening and beautiful testaments to God's fearsome creative gift. They are all titled with small brass plates. A lantern fly, closer to the size of a lantern than a fly, with two green wings and an even bigger second pair in translucent gold. A flower leaf hopper with a body the size of a chickadee and stretched out like Superman in flight. A moving leaf insect that looks just like a million oak leaves she has seen and never once considered might crawl away. A rhinoceros beetle as big as her hand and with beastly horns that give it its name. They are everywhere. Dinosaur like creatures. Every kind of butterfly. Giant moths. More beetles. Even a trail of army ants. Standing out against the white of one bookshelf is a scorpion that must be over six inches from stinger to claw. She can see her reflection in its black armor.

On and around the professor's cluttered desk are at least a dozen praying mantises: a rectangular acrylic paperweight, a framed display with several different types and sizes, a six-inch toy version with adjustable limbs, a wonderfully detailed pen and ink drawing of one called the false garden mantid. She can't resist picking up the paperweight and inspecting the creature suspended inside. Its front legs are no longer praying but spread and raised in surrender, its bug eyes staring out as if begging for release. June feels herself sinking into the mantis's desperate eyes. As often as she has seen these elegant insects in her garden, she has never *really* seen one. Not like this. And not the eyes. Half-domed, a million eyes rolled into one. Eyes in every direction. Eyes of a huntress. Eyes of a witness to more than she can ever comprehend. Was her last image that of her captor? Was she alive when she was dipped in this resin? What did she know in that moment?

The men's voices swell and break the mantis's spell. June carries the paperweight with her to the window. She pushes aside the curtain of the professor's bird blind. The waning moon is a ladle pouring white light over the silver maple. It glistens the leaves and spills into her yard, highlighting June's sleeping garden, her idle feeders. Her house, too, reflects its own moon-white. Her motionless porch swing with its dull porch light overhead. The delicate lace of her backlit curtains. She is witness to her own life. She places herself within the scene and feels a fondness for what she is seeing. The experience of being at once a part of and separate from her own life makes her profoundly aware of what she has been missing lately. Companionship. These are her neighbors. Their presence is validation. Their needs are confirmation. As she releases the curtain, she feels more at home than she has in months.

"June?" Cyril calls from the bottom of the stairs. "Pumpkin hour for me, kiddo."

June apologizes to the petrified mantis for disturbing her and replaces the paperweight. As she turns to leave, a drop of moonlight glints off a small object on the professor's desk. Silver with a cross in a red field. It seems to rise and hover above the desk like the spirit of itself. *Why do I know it?* June wonders.

She steps into the unlit hall, blinks back the apparition, and slowly descends.

∽

Rose is awakened by a dream.

She and her father are on his porch in Steamboat Springs staring into a sky made up of more light than dark. He quotes Einstein: *God is subtle, but he isn't malicious.*

She says, *Every god I've ever heard of is pretty damn vicious.*

He says, *I'm not talking about those little human gods. I'm talking about Nature. She's not trying to fool us. We don't understand her ways, so we think she has it in for us. But we do it to ourselves. We make life mean.*

*Oh yeah?* Rose says. *Well, look at me. At Kel. If this isn't malicious, then what is? These deaths are cruel. I'm not just watching myself die, I'm watching others watch me die. You went quickly, you lucky son of a bitch. You don't know what it's like to see the horror on people's faces when they see what's left of me. And what about Kel? Nature is disassembling him one brain cell at a time, like Jenga blocks. One more and he could crumble. If not Nature's, then whose cruelty is this?*

*And so it goes,* her father says. *What can you do about it?*

*Live,* Rose says. *Persist to spite Einstein's too-clever god. She can have her fun with me, but not Kel. Not my Kel,* she screams. And she is awake.

Kel is not next to her. She has no idea what time it is. She is sure he is with his bugs. His beloved bugs. She needs to talk to him. She needs to tell him it was a good night. She needs him to come to bed. To lie next to her and remember with her. To remember her flesh-colored flesh. Remember when her thighs commanded horses, her hands quieted fears, her scent drew butterflies, her voice filled rooms. She wants him to remember her. But her bell is out on the balcony.

She works her way out of bed, gathers her oxygen and cane. She's between worlds as she shuffles down the hall; the world of sleep with its defiance and indignation, and this breathless, daunting world with its linear time and damn gravity. Kel's office door is open. She makes her way slowly, at no time do her feet lose contact with the floor. She will surprise him. Standing outside the door she can see that only his desk light is on. His curtains are closed except for one panel next to where he is sitting in his armchair at the window. He doesn't notice her. He's deep in thought and is worrying something between his thumb and forefinger. It's small but catches the moonlight.

It's shiny, metallic. He's transfixed. She's as close as she can be without stepping into the room. She tries to make out what has him hypnotized. She shuffles one step closer and now she can see another lit window opposite Kel's. June's window. Her bedroom window.

# The Psychopathy Gambit

*Wednesday, May 20*

The silver pocketknife hadn't even crossed June's mind since the day Doug received it. He was never much for souvenirs, but when his brother-in-law gave one to each of his groomsmen, Doug had been impressed. It was sterling silver and engraved with his initials. "Not trivial," Doug had said after he examined the gift. Seeing the silver cross on Kelsey's desk reminded June that she had lost track of Doug's knife, a modest family heirloom, but not trivial. There are only a few places it could be. His bedside table. Maybe in his box of cufflinks, tie clips, and lapel pins she'd tucked away in a drawer. Maybe the catchall basket in the bathroom, or in with her jewelry. The junk drawer in the kitchen is a possibility. Or the fireproof box in the closet where she keeps important papers and some old coins.

But it wasn't in any of those places and now she's beginning to obsess about it. She calls Kevin and gets his voicemail.

"Hi, honey. I'm calling for a silly reason. I've misplaced something of your father's and I'm wondering if I gave it to you and forgot. It's a small silver Swiss Army knife with his initials on it. Not one of those big red ones with a bunch of tools. This one is thin and has a knife and a nail file for sure. Scissors, too, I think. Anyway, it's not an emergency. Whenever you get this just let me know, okay? Love to Bonnie and the kids. Bye."

The image of the silver cross on a shield-shaped red field is stuck in her head. So out of place among the mantises. Did she really see it? Kevin must have it. Or maybe it's in Doug's writing desk. She hasn't checked the writing desk yet.

❦

When Kel asks her to read his latest draft pages, Rose doesn't mention what she saw last night. Despite standing in the hall-way filled with a harpy's rage and an agonizing desire to throw something sharp at his head, she forced herself to retreat. *I'm still here!* she wanted to scream. But she clamped her jaw against it, stabbing her cane into the floor until the rage was sapped and all she could manage was to drag herself back to bed. Now she drops Kel's pages on her breakfast tray and lets her head fall back on her pillow.

"You didn't write this," she says.

He stops pacing in front of the French doors and speaks from across the room.

"What are you saying?"

"I said—you didn't write this."

"Of course I did."

"Kel, this is about Vikings. You're a bug man. This isn't you."

He approaches her with his hands out as if to plead his in-nocence. "The research is not mine, but its application to my study of these sly succubae, the recognition of its logic and its significance to understanding how mantis communities exhibit a sort of simplistic psychopathy is absolutely mine."

"So, praying mantises are—Viking warrior hawks?"

"There are parallels."

"You're being ridiculous."

"Can't you see it? The aberrant peacetime behavior of the Viking warriors and the deceitful signaling systems of distressed mantids."

"Little green psychopaths?"

Kel sits on the end of her bed. "Would it help if I read it to you?"

"How about I read it to you?" she says. "*People with this—'psychopath radar'—in effect have developed—an early warning system—allowing them to take—evasive action to avoid—interaction with people—who give them 'the creeps' —or make their 'skin crawl.'* These are people you're—talking about. You equate bugs to people—then back to bugs here—and say, *An individual—forsaking the tribe…*" Rose drops the pages again. "There is no mantis tribe, Kel. What's wrong with you?"

Kel's gaze is somewhere off to her right. He can't seem to align his eyes with hers. His eyes finally settle and he says, "I thought it was rather brilliant really. You don't know bugs as I know them. There's much more than meets the eye."

"Listen," Rose insists. "This is the only—sentence that matters. *If by producing—fewer eggs—a female is able to—significantly increase—pheromone signaling—and thereby—save her life—why wouldn't she?* Exactly. Why wouldn't she, Kel? She's a bug. Her every cell says—*live*. It's not psychopathic behavior—or as you call it—*a legitimate biological—survival gambit.*" Rose flips to the next page. "And then you write—this about the males. *Despite the heightened—pheromone production—of these distressed females—male mantids have not shown—any indication of—having developed a—form of mantid—'psychopath radar.'*" She drops the pages back into her lap and catches her breath. She doesn't know where Kel thinks he's headed with his harebrained thesis, but it doesn't matter to her anymore. He's unraveling and she sees no point in pretending. No point in believing he is capable of finding his way out of this ooze of liquifying thoughts. Her only option, she knows now, is to wade into the goop and pull him out.

"Mantid psychopath radar," she says. "Kel, you do realize—how crazy that sounds?"

Kel's head turns slowly toward her as if she has awakened him from a sound sleep. He stands and reaches for his pages. He tugs firmly until she surrenders them. He looks down at her, and says, "Not at all. This is aberrant behavior in need of an explanation. It makes perfect sense to look outside of the mantid's world for analogous anomalies."

"But human societies?" Rose says. "Sounds like you're joking. Unless…"

"Unless what?" he asks.

"Unless you're speaking—metaphorically. Your mantids standing in—for humans."

"Now that would be crazy."

"A bug-eat-bug world," Rose continues. "Every mantid for itself."

"That's good," Kel says. "I like that."

"But just a tad familiar, don't you think?"

"How do you mean?"

"Kel, please don't insult me."

Kel stands by the side of the bed, staring down at her with a look she reads as panic.

"You really don't see it, do you? The barren mantid—preying on her mate."

The weight of recognition buckles his knees, and Kel slumps onto the edge of the bed. "No," he moans. "You can't possibly think this has anything to do with us?"

Rose manages a more convincing facsimile of a laugh than she has been able to produce in months. "How can you sit there—and pretend it never—occurred to you? I understand if you feel—trapped." Rose taps the pages Kel clutches. "I would admire this—as a piece of noir fiction. A little twee perhaps—but entertaining. But as science? Please."

Rose can see that Kel is dumbstruck, perhaps even frightened. She wonders if she's getting through to him. *Will he come to see what I see? Will he realize how twisted his mind has become?*

But all he says is, "Maybe you should rest."

Rose presses on. "What do you see when you—sit in the dark staring—at her window?"

Being discovered seems to draw his face down like melting wax. She knows he knows she knows, but all he can manage is a pitiful, "What are you talking about?"

"Oh, please," she spits. "Last night—staring at her window—a moonstruck child. What are you thinking, Kel? That June will care for you?"

"Stop it. I don't know what you're talking about."

"I saw you in your chair. Staring out the window. What were you staring at—if not her?"

"You," he says without hesitation, without a hint of shame. "I see only you."

"God, you're pathetic. Snap out of it. Can't you see—what's happening to you? I didn't stick around—all these years just to—watch you slip into—lunacy."

"It's true." Kel leans confidently toward her as if his truth is a shield. "It's always you. Why are you acting like this? I choose you. Always you."

She places her cool hand on his inflamed face. "Oh, Kel. Sweet, brilliant Kel. If only you could—understand how—hard it is—to see you like this. I'm tired now. Take your fiction. Go back to your bug people."

He stands at the foot of the bed in helpless suspension before lowering his head and slowly, step by tortured step, de-materializing. Rose sinks into her pillows and lets her eyes close. *How many deaths do I have to live through?*

෬

June doesn't usually screen her calls. She doesn't get that many. But she lets the machine pick up this one because she has gardening gloves on and is in the middle of transplanting her herbs. When she hears, "Hey, Mom, got your message. I don't have the knife, but I'm really calling to talk about—" she scrambles out of her gloves, shakes off the dirt, and snatches the phone from its cradle.

"Kevin honey, it's me," she says too loudly. "I'm here. Sorry, I was up to my elbows in potting soil."

"Hi, Mom. How are you?"

He sounds refreshingly eager to talk to her. "Great, really good," she says. "Even better hearing your voice. You sound cheery."

"So do you. Bonnie and I were a little worried after your message."

"Worried? What about?" Kevin has some distinctive charac-ter traits, but worrying, especially about her, is not one of them.

"I don't know," he says. "You just sounded kind of down, maybe a little lonely. The whole looking for Dad's pocketknife thing."

"I suppose that could come off as wistful. I just happened to see one like it and it made me realize I hadn't seen your dad's for a while. I looked for it but couldn't turn it up. No big thing. I just thought maybe you might know."

"Sorry," he says.

"It's nothing, really," June says, and buries her disappointment at not having solved the mystery. It had been comforting to think that Kevin had the knife.

"So, are we going to be able to talk you into coming to see us soon? It's been six months. We're all settled in. Guest room is waiting."

June carries the phone outside, sits on her gardening bench, and deadheads the browning irises. "I'd really like to. I know I should be better about traveling on my own after all these years."

"Mom, I'm sorry to ask, but have you been taking your medication?"

His voice sounds genuinely caring. Kevin is like Doug that way. A good heart. She hopes his turns out to be more resilient than his dad's.

"I take it when I need it," she says. "It can make me nauseous. I'm not sure what's worse, the blues or the blahs."

"Are you getting out? Meeting people?"

This aspect of his concern is decidedly un-Doug-like and less appealing to her. She knows he wants what he thinks is best for her. June can't blame him for not being able to understand that he is the only man whose well-being interests her.

"You sound like Doctor Price," she says. "You shouldn't worry about me. I'm fine."

"But we do worry. Fifty-seven is young. And it's so easy to meet people these days."

"The truth is, I'm not terribly interested in new people. I have my birders and church, and there's the garden and the animals. Jonesy and I keep plenty busy."

"Well, that's good. I was beginning to think you were turning into a hermit. Wondering if we should start calling you Saint June?"

"Very funny. Stick with Mom, please."

"Saint Mom then?"

June sighs deeply and he hears.

"Sorry," he says. "I'll stop bugging you."

"You're not bugging me."

"Mom, I'm sorry, but I've gotta go. Bonnie needs help with Cameron. I can't tell which one of them is shrieking at the moment. Please think about a visit."

"I will."

"Love you."

"You too, dear."

And he is gone. "Dear? Good Lord," June says. "I sound so old. Do mothers even say *dear* to their adult children anymore?" Thinking about their conversation, she concludes that he's right. She should go visit. She should go soon. She needs to go. But right now there is the small matter of Doug's knife.

"I remember," Kelsey says to his window. *Last night I sat in this same chair staring into the infinite black, out to where a billion suns can be blotted out by a single thumb. I was threading gaps like a child playing connect the dots with the stars. Trying to reconstruct the details that once ignited the shadows. I lose details every day now, but I know they're still there. Details buried under bundles of brain waste that swell like the ocean's garbage patches. The details don't disappear just because I can't see them. The green beetle on the spathe of an aubergine calla lily spreads its pollen despite my clouded eyes. So, yes, I was staring into the waste-filled void. I was searching what is left of me. And all I could see—all I can see playing among the hundred billion neurons is Rose. My beautiful grandiflora dancing among the sagebrush of Colorado's steppe. I take her hand that first time, and she holds mine like a mother does, leading and pulling ever so gently. She walks me into her breathless world, her majestic, mountainous, unforgiving world. I float on her thin air. Gasp for breath as she runs me through the mile-high shrubland. I am hers. She is no one's. And when she leaves, I am hopeless. And when she returns—and she always returns—hope returns. She takes me back. And I am retaken.*

"What will you want of me this time, my desert Rose?" he says. "What's left of me to take?"

# DETAILS

*Thursday, May 21*

On the return leg of their morning walk, June coaxes Jonesy to take their longer route home. She needs more time to think things through. Jonesy isn't particularly enthusiastic and stops at the pivotal corner that marks the difference between a five- and a fifteen-minute walk home. It's a cool morning and the air is dry, but cloud cover and the absence of even a hint of a breeze adds a heaviness to the day. Regardless, June needs the extra time. So, when sweet talk doesn't unstick him, she gives the leash a firm tug and Jonesy complies. They leave the sidewalk and take the path through the few wooded acres of Marrsville whose preserved-open-space designation has kept them out of the clutches of developers. The second-growth trees and dense ferns trap the dew and add to the morning's melancholy.

The extra time is not changing her mind. She's convinced she needs to see for herself. She has another visit planned with Rose later today. She'll find an opportunity to slip into the professor's office. The only complication is that she doesn't want either Rose or the professor to know what she's doing. It would be impossible to explain. She will have to pick a time when Rose is resting, and the professor is occupied outside of his office. It shouldn't be difficult. A few seconds are all she will need to put the mystery to rest. *I just need to be patient. There's no rush. It's just sitting there on the desk.*

The simplicity of the plan is calming. As they follow the path's loop back up to the street, the sun burns a hole through the clouds and begins evaporating the mustiness of the woods and lifting the morning's weight. *An omen,* June decides. *Before the day is over, I'll know.*

ᕔ

Kelsey can't return to his paper with his mind preoccupied with Rose's suspicions. The more he thinks about her comments, the more he finds himself sucked in by her take on the work. She has poisoned the well. He can't decide if he should abandon the project altogether or give the poison time to work its way through his thought process. In the meantime, he has an idea that might at least allow him to reconcile with Rose over the disrespect she felt he exhibited the other night. He is convinced she will not believe the truth of what played out in his mind as he stared into the night sky. His only hope is to earn her forgiveness. He's pulling out of the driveway to go buy the gift he believes will win Rose back when June waves him down. She walks around to the driver's side, and he lowers his window.

"Hi," she says. "Is Rose awake?"

June is casual and familiar now. The novelty of her presence in his life is gone and with it the unnerving thrill he used to experience when she approached. He is aware of what has been lost and grateful for its passing. His response is equally familiar and without circumspection.

"She was awake enough a minute ago to toss me out," he says.

"Toss you out?"

"We had a quarrel. I'm off to buy her a gift in hopes of mending the fence."

"I'm sorry to hear that. I know it's earlier than usual, but do you think she would like company?"

"She used being tired as part of her reason for excusing me, but you're welcome to try. The back door should be open."

"Are you sure you're okay to drive?" June asks. "I could take you."

"Thank you, but I believe I can do this." He presses the window button and it closes as he backs away.

&#8766;

Rose hears the car leave. *Off to buy me a gift, no doubt. As if stuff can save us now. What is it with men? A gift and all is forgiven. All is forgotten. Pitifulness must be packed on the Y chromosome. Can't he see it's too late for presents? No need to chime in, Dad. I already know how you feel. I need to talk to my neighbor.*

Rose closes her eyes and whispers to the empty room. "Come to me, my Geraldine. Innocent anchoress—waiting under the—broad-breasted oak. Sweet foil to my fading. Where are you? Tu-woo, tu-woo, tu-woo! Come, rival neighbor saint. Come to the one who's—lost her glamor, is losing her man. Come to me. I have use for you. Hear me."

❧

June watches the professor turn onto the main road before heading for the back door. She enters quietly so as not to wake Rose if she is sleeping. If she is not sleeping, June hopes to be quiet enough that she can duck unnoticed into the professor's office before visiting with her. She's not expected, so she can take her time.

The house is quiet except for the now familiar ticktock of the living room mantel clock. The lone sound seems amplified by the otherwise grave silence. June uses its rhythm to time her steps, synchronizes herself to its pulse. Tick for the left foot, tock for right. The air in the stairwell drifts up, warming as she climbs. At the top of the stairs she notices the sun has found the second-floor hallway through the open door of the guest bedroom. The professor's office door is open too, his curtains closed. Being on the north side of the house, as the sun follows its slight southeasterly arc, the drawn curtains cast the office in a weird late-morning twilight.

June hears nothing from Rose's room, so she steps into the office and pushes the door all but closed. She expects the knife to be where she last saw it. It's not. She looks over the entire desktop, pats the scattered papers. Was it a hallucination? Has she played a cruel joke on herself? No, she's convinced it's here. She reaches for the desk drawer and bumps the professor's rolling chair. It rattles. She stops and listens for Rose to react. She hears only her own heart pounding and the muted ticktock from downstairs. There's no sound of movement, no labored breathing. June gently pulls the top desk drawer's two brass handles and it glides open. Paper clips, tacks, nail clipper, scissors, staples, stationary, letter opener, drawing compass. The search is taking more than the anticipated few seconds. June settles herself, tries to slow her heart and her movements. She deliberately scans the room for other logical places the knife could be. There's a shelf in the lamp table by the chair, but no knife. She checks the bookcases. Lifts the couch cushions. Shoves her hands down the sides of the armchair. She stands back and surveys again. She decides she needs more light. She pulls back the curtains. There! On the windowsill. A silver cross on a red field. It's real. She picks it up and can feel markings on the back. June closes her eyes and turns the knife over in her hand.

*She's here,* Rose thinks. *I can feel her. But where? Why doesn't she come to me?*

"June?" she calls out.

There's no answer. Rose is sure her voice is just too weak to carry all the way to wherever June is. She wonders what her neighbor could be up to. Rose isn't interested in tea on the patio or some other surprise cooked up by the co-conspirators. She decides to find her, to disrupt any scheme they may be plotting.

*I can still do this,* Rose prompts herself, though there's weakness now where just days before there was the approximation of strength. *Breathe,* she tells herself. *No need to hurry. Breathe. She's close. The sound is nothing more than a fluttering of tiny wings, but I hear her. There it is again. Kel's office. If I didn't know better, I'd say a soffit sparrow flew in the window again. But I do know better. It's her. What's she doing?*

"June?" Rose manages between steps. Still there's no response. "June." She nudges the door with her cane. There's no response. The door slowly sways back toward her. Rose jabs her cane harder into the door. It swings open and stays. June is sitting in Kel's armchair, her hands cupped before her like she's praying.

"What are you doing?" Rose asks.

"He stole it," June says.

"What are you—talking about?"

"Doug's knife." June parts her hands and reveals a small silver pocketknife. "He stole it."

June looks just as baffled by her own discovery as Rose is. "Stole a pocketknife? From where?"

"My house."

"He was in your house?"

"He must have been."

"How could he have been—in your house—without you knowing?"

June looks like she's trying to convince herself that her story makes sense. "I don't know."

"Then why do you—think he stole it?"

"Because it's here. I just found it. It has Doug's initials on it." Her voice is as thin as Rose's, puffed words, as if she can't quite catch her breath. "I'm sorry," June says." I saw it on his desk Tuesday night. I didn't believe it then. But I had to know."

"I don't care about—the fucking knife," Rose says.

June stiffens. "What?"

"I don't care," Rose repeats, and drops into the creaking desk chair. "All that matters is—you see how he is. I've been trying to tell you. My husband's—losing his mind."

"I'm so sorry, Rose. I didn't know. I didn't see."

"I don't want—I can't watch him—fall apart."

"We can get him help," June says. "You don't have to do this alone."

"I won't watch him die—this way."

"Die? Rose, Kelsey could live many more years, and happily."

"Happily?" Rose hisses. "Alone. Mindless."

"I'm sorry. I didn't mean it like that. Let me take him to see a doctor. We'll get a diagnosis, proper treatment. While you can still be part of it."

Rose sits silently, as if considering June's suggestion, then says, "I've seen this."

"Seen what?" June asks.

"This death. When the mind goes. I don't want to—be a part of it."

"Rose, we don't know what this is."

"I know. I've seen it."

For several minutes they sit together in the office's untimely twilight without speaking. June is no stranger to dementia. As a church volunteer, she's seen people who walk around with permanent smiles in rapt wonder at the countless mysteries that make up every moment. For others, their dying brain is a ceaseless torment, a living purgatory. June would never wish that on anyone. But even with this knowledge, she senses Rose's dread is something darker than the worst of what June has witnessed. She turns the small knife over and over in her hand, trying to decide what to say. Should she ask what Rose is talking about? Address it directly. Or focus on the professor, on trying to convince Rose to let her help him? And there's the option to say nothing. To settle for rescuing her keepsake and to let Rose do the rest. *We are our burdens*, she thinks. *They are only lifted after we cease to be.*

Rose watches June worry the knife. That such a petty incident could deliver her to this moment makes Rose question her belief in free will. What are the odds that of all the little knickknacks Kel could pilfer he would choose something that has such great significance? And then compound that improbability with the odds of June seeing it and fixating on it. Impossible. When Rose was a young woman, she feared she had inherited her mother's genes. That her mind, too, would slowly melt in her fifties. And if that were to happen, she told herself, she would not want to be with a man like her father; a man who would give her over to the care of others so that he would not have to give himself over to her. When she met Kel, it wasn't love at first sight. He was awkward, as if he didn't realize how long his arms or legs were. When he reached, he reached through objects, knocking them over, scattering them. When he walked, he often stumbled, as if the rest of his body anticipated a longer stride and he'd gotten ahead of himself. She sometimes felt his physical development had never progressed beyond adolescence. For all his awkwardness, as she came to know him, what she noticed was his attention to detail. She intuited that it would make him a caring partner, an attentive if somewhat clumsy lover. She also noticed the immediacy of his attention: that it was taken by what was in front of him, not, like her father, by what or who might be over the next rise. If she kept him close, she was certain, he would fix his attention on her. He would be loyal and not leave her when she most needed him. Happily, her mind did not begin to melt when she crossed into her fifties. Instead it would be her cancer that tested Kel, a disease that left her wits intact, preserving her power to choose. All this time she had been focused on taking control of her own end, on unburdening Kel and choosing the death she desired when her time came. But now, everything has changed. Kel needs her. She is no longer convinced she can control their fates. Her mind races through questions. Is this woman to be my relief? Is this who Kel will come to know when he has forgotten me? Will his mind twist June into me or will I become June? Who will Kel become?

Rose watches until June feels her gaze and looks up from the glinting, impossible object cradled in her hands. June sits up as if she is going to renew her appeal on Kel's behalf, but before she can speak, Rose says, "Dr. Bernstein. At Penn Medicine."

June closes her fist around the knife and shoves it in her pocket. She leaves her chair to find a pen and a scrap of paper on Kel's desk.

"The university's hospital in the city?" she asks.

"Their med center—in Rivertown."

"I know it," June says.

"Take him to see—Geoffrey Bernstein."

June makes her notes. "This is good," she says. "You'll see."

"Let's get out of here," Rose says. "Wait for Kel—on the deck."

"Let me help you up."

As June lifts Rose out of the chair, Rose grasps June's shoulders and looks her directly in the eyes. She steadies herself and says firmly, "I refuse to watch."

"I understand, Rose. I do. Let me help you to the deck, then I'll call the doctor's office."

Rose is not convinced June fully understands what she is saying. But it can wait. It's all conjecture now. They'll talk again when they know more.

∽

Rose is with June on the deck when Kelsey returns. "I've brought you a surprise," he announces, as he lopes across the bedroom. "Look what I found. Cyril's book. *Morning Songs.* It's an audio guide with recordings of over a hundred birdsongs." He flips through the book and stops at a familiar page. "Listen to the cardinal." He presses the button below the small speaker attached to the book. "Marvelous, isn't it? So clear. Beautiful recordings. I've heard that song so many times and never matched it with its source. It requires a musical ear to remember such associations. I wish I were more musical."

He stops his presentation and awaits Rose's reaction. She is looking at him with great interest but, it seems to Kelsey, she is directing none of that interest toward the book. She glances over at June, who seems to receive Rose's look as a cue. June clears her throat and reaches into her pocket. She removes a small silver object and places it on the sunflower table.

"Professor," June asks, "do you recognize this?"

Kelsey takes a closer look at the pocketknife he discovered in his own pocket not long ago. "I do. I found that recently. Why do you ask?"

Rose turns back to Kelsey. When she speaks, he hears a voice as cool and dry as a desert night. "Do you remember—where you found it?"

"I don't. Unless you'll accept my pants pocket as an answer."

"June tells me you—stole it from her house." Rose's eyes are unblinking, her pupils widening to suck in more light.

"Well—" June interjects, as if she intends to soften the accusation.

Rose interrupts. "Did you?"

"Stole? How could I have stolen it? From whom?"

"Think, Kel. Did you go into—June's house when—she wasn't there?"

"June's house? Of course not—" Kelsey starts his denial, but he can't finish. His mind is flooded with images—puzzle, pictures, paintings, books, flowers, pillows, bras, pie, pictures, pictures, pictures—but he can't place them. What is he seeing?

"Kel."

"I'm trying." He's dizzy and squeezes his eyes shut to stop the sudden vertigo. Fireworks of phosphenes project onto the back of his eyelids. Glorious electric mums. Multiple blooms at once. And colors. Bright, searing colors. And sparks like a sudden summer rain in full sunlight. Sparks enough to fill the gaps. All the missing light—

✧

"Kel!" Rose snaps, and his eyes open. "Where did you find it?"

"Find it?"

"The knife. That knife." She points at the table.

Kel becomes suddenly distant. Rose senses him moving away from her like a kite spinning out string. "I don't remember," he says, a confession that seems to astonish him as much as it does her.

"Think," Rose says.

"I am and I can't—"

"Think!"

"I'm trying."

"Professor," June says, "I thought I saw it recently in my living room on the desk. Does that sound right?"

Rose watches Kel's face relax at the sound of June's more patient voice. *A moment ago, he looked like he was having a bad dream. Now he's back in the room with us and having a conversation. If not madness, then what?*

"I believe it was upstairs," he says. "Yes, that's right. In a basket. Does that make sense?"

June says, "The basket in the linen closet."

"Yes. A rich repository of artifacts. At the bottom."

"What were you doing there?" Rose asks.

Kelsey turns to her as if he's just noticed that she's in the room. "Looking," he says.

"For what?"

"Details."

"Details?"

"Yes. Details."

"What does that mean, Professor?" June asks.

"Things you can't know without seeing them for yourself."

"What did you see?" Rose asks.

"Family. Pupa, nymphs, adults."

The three of them sit in dizzying silence. Kel looks from one face to the other as if expecting someone to speak. Rose nods at June.

"Professor, Rose and I have been talking and we think it's time for you to see Dr. Bernstein."

"Geoffrey?" Kel says cheerily. "Whatever for?"

"Just a checkup," June says. "Rose told me you haven't been in for a while, and since she can't accompany you, I offered to drive you over."

Kel looks at Rose for what she assumes is confirmation that she approves of this arrangement.

"It's a good idea," Rose says. "You haven't been—yourself lately."

"Not myself?" Kel seems amused by the suggestion. "I'm feeling in the pink, actually. Your perking up this spring has cheered me too. Not sure what all this fuss is about."

Rose leans forward in her chair. "Kel, you broke into—June's house."

"Well, broke in might be a little harsh," June says.

Rose admires June's diplomacy, her calm. *I used to be able to show such patience and steadiness with the kids. My horses also were good at instilling calm. Maybe I'm being too harsh, spooking Kel, sparking his crazy.* She settles back in her chair and allows June to take the lead.

"We're concerned about some of the things you've done and about the forgetting," June explains. "It's probably nothing, but Dr. Bernstein can run some tests and then we'll know. We were fortunate to get an appointment for tomorrow."

Kel turns from June to Rose. "If it will put your mind at ease, my dear, I will happily chat with Geoffrey."

"Dear heart," Rose says, "it's not my mind—I'm worried about."

# Non posso vivere senza di te

*Tuesday, May 26*

As June makes her way upstairs with the tea tray, she becomes aware of a weariness that wasn't present even moments before. The stress of the last week suddenly assumes physical weight and walking that weight up the Geddes's staircase seems, for the first time, like labor. It has been a hard week for Rose. She hasn't been complaining of more pain than usual or taking more pills. But since learning of Kelsey's trespass, she has been dispirited. June's take on it is that Rose is even more upset by Kelsey's intrusion than June is. Of course, June was shaken by the professor's actions and troubled by the indication that he probably needs more supervised care. But there hasn't been another incident even remotely comparable that either she or Rose know about. June has kept close tabs on the professor during the week, accompanying him to the grocery store, even allowing him to drive so she could see how he was doing in that department. He drives slowly, which she is sure bothers other drivers more than it bothers her. They made it to the store without incident. And he seemed quite comfortable shopping, though he is a bit of a hostage to his routine. He insists on making his way through the aisles in a particular order, which she considers another good sign. She had anticipated that he would be easily distracted, impulsive, even disoriented, but he stuck to his list and remained on task. Her conversations with him over the last several days have been no less animated than usual. The professor was contrite immediately following the confrontation, but he seems to have moved on. And so has June. The weariness she feels now stems from Rose's inability to do the same. Despite having received what June perceives to be a hopeful diagnosis from Dr. Bernstein, Rose cannot let it go. June reported that Dr. Bernstein's exam still indicates age-related cognitive decline. June stressed that this was good news. Nothing else out of the ordinary. When Kelsey admitted that he had issues remembering things now and then, had gotten himself confused in the car a few times, and didn't remember much about the pocketknife incident, Dr. Bernstein was understandably concerned. He asked if the professor's attention drifted off at times or if he'd experienced any hallucinations. June told Rose that Kelsey had freely admitted to seeing things. June confessed that the hallucinations surprised her, but that it made sense considering some of the things Kelsey has said to her. It explained why his attention wanders now and then. She explained that Dr. Bernstein decided he would run a couple of other blood tests to rule out any vitamin deficiencies or an infection. June also passed along what she considered hopeful news. Dr. Bernstein had talked to her and Kelsey about pathological grief. Rose had rolled her eyes at the phrase. But June thinks it's a real possibility. Dr. Bernstein explained that the symptoms Kelsey described were things that people who have suffered great loss can experience when they have trouble dealing with their grief.

"You've been dying for what, over two years? It's possible Kelsey began grieving your loss when he first brought you home," June had told Rose. "You've beaten the odds by living as long as you have, but that hasn't changed your prognosis. Kelsey lives every day knowing you could die at any moment. He knows how hard this has been on you. You must have a sense of how hard it's been for him."

Rose had been unmoved. "Pathological grief is just—another way of saying—he's going crazy."

"If the professor is crazy, it's because he's crazy about you."

Rose had responded by telling June she was tired and wanted to be left alone for the rest of the day. The days since then have felt like an endless attempt on June's part to drag Rose out of her funk, her own pathological self-pity.

Now, as she approaches Rose, June picks up their conversation where they left off when she went downstairs to get the tea. She tries to be patient, finding it harder to disguise her exasperation at repeating information Rose has heard several times. Each time she tells it, she tries a slightly different spin. So far, Rose has remained resolutely glum.

"Keep in mind," June tries yet again, "Kelsey was so clear-headed during the exam that Dr. Bernstein considered him competent enough to sign a document that gives the doctor permission to talk to me about the results of the tests. That's a big deal."

"He was performing," Rose says. "He was probably—showing off for you."

*Now,* June thinks, *she's crossed the line. This is not about me. I refuse to let this be about me.* "Rose, are we still talking about Kelsey?" Her voice scolds. June doesn't apologize for her parental tone. "I hope we are, because he and I had a very encouraging doctor's visit, and he's had several good days since then. Still you insist on seeing only the negative, refusing to take anything positive from what I've been telling you. Honestly…"

Rose puts her cup down and grips the edge of the table with her gray blue hands. She looks as if she wants to upend the table, like she'd throw it over the deck railing if she had the strength.

"Positive? You want positive? I'm positive I'm dying. I'm positive Kel is going—batshit crazy. I'm positive—you don't get it."

June quiets herself and considers how to respond. It's becoming increasingly difficult for her to feel charitably toward Rose. All this gloom and anger. She's beginning to think it may be time to bring in professional help. Let someone at least get paid to subject themselves to these outbursts. The professor may be batshit crazy, but his crazy is much more pleasant than Rose's dying. *What a horrible thing to think.* June decides that before she loses patience and begins to say such thoughts out loud, a more prudent approach is to find the professor and send him to sit with his distraught wife.

∽

At June's urging, Kelsey wanders down the hall from his office to check on Rose. Since June has been visiting nearly every day, there hasn't been any bell ringing lately. Now he goes to Rose either when he is encouraged by June or, occasionally, when he decides he needs to see her, to be reassured that she is still with him. The bell had been a reminder that Rose wanted or needed him. With June around and Rose back to spending nearly all her wakeful time in bed, she wants and needs him less now. He had hoped that as there was less life in her, less time for her, she would want more of him. But his presence no longer seems to comfort her. When he is away from her and unable to distract himself with some busywork or with his writing, he finds he is spending much of his time trying to reconcile his feelings of sadness and relief. The sadness he does not question. But the relief and its ameliorating effect on the sadness, this is what he is trying to grasp. Until June began providing the relief, he had been unaware of how heavily Rose's needs pressed on him. Not the needs themselves so much as the effort in meeting them. Daily tasks of cooking, cleaning, shopping, bathroom breaks, and bathing that not so long ago were sources of dutiful pleasure, or if not pleasure then at least moments of usefulness and purpose, have become drone-like work. He finds it curious that he feels this now that the work isn't all left to him. When it is his turn, he is fully aware of the effort required; he consciously experiences the giving over of himself to Rose. It brings to mind the matriphagy of crab spiders, of the mother's sacrifice for her young. He grins at his gruesome analogy. *What I'm doing isn't that,* he reminds himself. *I mean, what have I really sacrificed?*

"Come closer," Rose says from her seat at the sunflower table. "Someone is mowing. I can't hear you."

"It was nothing, dear," Kel says, and joins her on the deck. "I was talking to myself. Thinking out loud."

"Hmm," Rose says, and gives him a look that tells him she knows exactly what he said.

He picks up his monologue as if she sits alongside him in his head, hears every word he speaks to himself and needs no context or clarification.

"Thinking about this process we're going through, I'm wondering what I, the one who is not dying, have sacrificed?" He touches the side of the teapot, feels the contents have cooled and decides not to pour himself a cup. "Caregiving is spoken of as a tremendous sacrifice. Caregivers are told to make sure they take time to care for themselves. That what we are doing can be difficult, burdensome. But what are we doing that is so different from what a mother does? Are mothers reminded to care for themselves because of the sacrifice motherhood demands of them? Only by marketers of mother-pampering products. The lotions and bath salts and spa treatments. But caregivers, those who care for those who once cared for themselves, we are told our efforts are onerous, taxing, draining. That we must seek relief or risk burning out. But how is what I am doing sacrifice? Did you and I not vow for better or worse until death?"

"This is what you're—thinking about?"

"Yes. That and what I'll prepare for lunch today."

"Let's talk about the—until death part."

Kelsey leans his forearms on the table and laces his fingers. "I'm sorry, I didn't mean to suggest... What I meant was that this is part of the bargain we couples strike when we state our vows, is it not? This isn't sacrifice, it's sacrament. A rite more important than the moment at the altar, because that promise is made in the abstract. Two delirious young people agreeing to something they know nothing about. But this. This is the real deal, so to speak. This is the promise manifest."

Rose raises her hand to stop him. "Lovely, dear. But that's not what I meant. I've been thinking too. And I think—it's time."

"Time, *tesoro mio*?" Kelsey tracks the word *time* through his mind and watches it sull like a barn-sour horse, refusing to move on. He tries to animate it with a couple of heels to the ribs, but this pony is not time as we know it—an inexorable forward plod of indefinite duration. No, this is a singular moment in time. The end of time. The terror.

"Kel, are you all right?"

"Sorry, dear. You were saying?"

"I said, would you mind terribly—if I died now."

Kelsey stands up. His chair flips backward and clatters on the deck. "Right this minute?"

"No. Calm down. Pick up the chair. Sit."

Kelsey composes himself and listens as Rose's blunt, broken sentences review her last several weeks. Good days, she calls them. Better than she had any right to expect. She speaks of her affection for June and how the spring has been the most temperate and lovely in recent memory. But she is tired now, and the pain, when it comes, is more difficult despite what her stoicism suggests. She doesn't want to drag him and now June through the inevitable. "There's no sense in that," she says. "I don't want to—experience it and—I'm sure you two—don't either." Before Kelsey can express his thoughts on what he does or does not want, Rose says, "But there's more to—my decision. An even more selfish reason."

She describes her experience of him. She portrays a befuddled old man whose antics betray a mind clutching at dissociated straws. A man whose life is a collection of fragments. Unfinished thoughts. Crazy writing. Abandoned projects. Aborted journeys. "I can't watch," she says. "The body is one thing. The mind another. I've seen both. Even a broken body has—choice, will. An addled brain…" She stops there, catches her breath and says, "I love you, Kel. But I can't stay—with you any longer. My heart can't bear it."

And she is quiet. She looks across the table at him with the closest approximation of affection that her death mask can manage. He returns a look he hopes communicates the same affection he holds for her, but after processing her description of him, he can't be certain what she sees when she looks across the table. A junk bug, maybe. The larval lacewing, head swaying haphazardly under a weight of its own creation, a body laden with carcasses. He says, "I love you too, *cuore mio. Non posso vivere senza di te.*"

She smiles. "You've been practicing. What did you say?"

ॐ

June allows the professor to handle the bulk of the lunch preparation. They decided to reheat the pasta fagioli June made for dinner on Friday and warm up a baguette. Kelsey is stirring the soup lazily when he says, "You're a woman of nature. Maybe you can help me sort this out. What I'm struggling with now is why she doesn't die?"

June crosses her arms and leans a hip into the counter. "I don't understand," she says.

Kelsey doesn't turn around. He's adjusting the aluminum foil tent over the baguette. "Neither do I," he says. He opens the oven, places the bread on the rack, closes the oven, returns to stirring the soup and says, "I've been preoccupied with divining an evolutionary explanation for how the female of the species developed its survival strategy. I can accept that, even at the cellular level, life demonstrates many fierce and dispassionate survival mechanisms. Introduce those cells to the most basic hindbrain neuronal network and their life-obsessed mechanisms naturally become more species-specific. What I can't grasp is why the mantis's mechanism of pumping up pheromone production in hopes of attracting a meal doesn't kill her."

The professor stops his stirring and looks to June as if they have been collaborators on his article from the beginning. She shrugs her confusion and says, "I'm going to need a little more information if you're expecting me to say anything even remotely helpful."

His face registers something between impatience and profound disappointment. "We've been at this for a while now. I thought you were paying attention."

June decides the more gracious of the options available to her is to play along. "I'm sorry. I've been distracted. Remind me where we left off."

Kelsey sighs heavily. "It isn't where we left off, but rather where we began. She's in extremis. Starving to death. In order to draw a male away from the other robust females in the vicinity, she must use what little life force she has left to produce the greatest amount of pheromone she can and then hope a male finds her. Why doesn't the effort kill her? Or, if not kill her, how does it not render her physically incapable of executing her assault on her unwitting victim?"

June squares herself up and attempts to mimic Kelsey's professorial airs. "I'm surprised, Professor. All these years of studying insects and you're still astonished by their powers. Just the other day I was reading that an ant's neck can support pressure up to five thousand times its body weight. How can we mere humans ever understand how that's possible?"

Kelsey looks to be considering her question, taking several moments to construct his response. He turns, gives the soup another absentminded stir and says, "Five thousand, is it now? Remarkable."

"Better check the bread," June suggests.

# BETTER DRUGS

*Saturday, May 30*

"Dying is hard," Rose says. "I need help."

June places the morning's pills and fresh juice on Rose's tray. "Then it's time we called in professional hospice care."

"I don't want some stranger—hovering over me."

"Rose, please forgive me. And don't take this the wrong way, but I'm tired of arguing with you about this."

"Then stop arguing and—help me."

June sits on the end of the bed. "Do we have to go through this every day?"

"Help me."

"Do you want me to stop coming over?"

"Help me."

"I'm not going to force you to eat or drink. But unless you tell me to stop coming over, I'm not going to stop bringing you your meals. You eat, you drink, that's your choice."

"Starving's too slow. Too hard. If I were a dog would—you starve me?"

June closes her eyes and folds her hands in her lap. She considers praying but doesn't know what to pray for. Death? A miracle cure? Her own release from the burden she's taken on?

"Don't you dare—pray for me," Rose says.

"Mind if I pray for me?"

"Humph. Only if you pray—to be rid of me."

June lets go of her spine and shoulders and sinks further into the bed. It's as if Rose can see the thoughts scrolling across her forehead. She hates what the embrace of death has done to Rose. She hates herself for wanting to be done with this as much as Rose does. She hates not knowing how long she will have to battle these hatreds, to ward off the despair they are beginning to cast over her life. After a long silence, June says, "Rose, have you ever considered how hard your dying has been on your husband, on me?"

Rose looks away, focusing her gaze on the canopy of neighborhood trees set against the cloudless southern sky. She echoes June's silence.

June thinks she has been too direct in her own defense. As she considers how to back away from the question she has left dangling between them, Rose is first to speak.

"I talked to Kel. He understands—I want to die."

"And I understand and I'm so sorry—"

"Don't be sorry. Help me."

"Rose, I won't help you die."

"Send the boy," Rose says.

"The boy? What boy?"

"Your boy. Reddish hair. Wiry. Sideburns."

"Big Joe?"

"If you say so."

"Send Joe. Why?"

"A better drug," Rose says.

June stands as if preparing to leave. She shakes her head. "I don't know what you're talking about."

"Morphine not reliable. I've seen it. Too slow."

"Rose, stop. I have no idea what you're getting at—"

"Good. Better that way. Send the boy. He'll know."

"Rose, I—"

Rose interrupts. "Are the boys—coming today?"

"I don't know. Maybe. It doesn't matter—"

"I'm not asking—you to kill me. I'm asking you—send the boy."

"Don't be like this." June's voice cracks under Rose's relentless insistence. Her weakening settles Rose. As if enchanted dust is being sprinkled over her, first her eyes close and then her mouth relaxes into serene neutrality. Her shoulders drop and she sinks into her pillows, her hands are like two small birds alighting in her lap. She looks as if she's meditating. *Is this dying?* June wonders. Rose's breath is shallow and steady.

"Rose?" June says, quietly so as not to wake her.

Rose's eyes remain closed, her body relaxed, her face serene. Just her lips move and the softest whisper escapes them. "Send the boy."

～

"You don't want to have anything to do with this," Cyril says. "If she wants to die, tell her to take it up with her doctor."

"You know that won't help," June says. "Not in Pennsylvania."

"That's her problem." He plants his hands on his hips in an act of desperate bravado. "Look, you don't want to do this. This isn't you."

"It's like a weird test. Like God is trying me for some reason."

"June, honey, it's not a test. It's a dying woman's desperate request. You don't have to make this out to be any more than that. She's asked you to do something she never should have asked."

"She has lung cancer," June says. "It's in her brain. She's in pain. She's convinced her husband is demented and is going to die a death more horrifying than her own. She's desperate. I could never live like that. She has no one else."

"Stop," Cyril says. "Sit down." He stands behind her and strokes her hair. "Listen to what you're doing. Why are you talking yourself into this?"

"I'm not really. I'm just saying—"

"Listen. Let's say this kid is who she thinks he is and can get her—whatever—and she uses it to kill herself. The police are going to want to know where she got the drugs."

"We don't even know if Joe can get them," June says. "Rose just wants to talk to him."

Cyril takes an impatient breath that tells June he's trying to find new words to say what he has already said but in a way that will change her mind. He glances out the window at the boys filling the wheelbarrow with a mix of top soil and peat and dumping it in the raised bed. "Look, the cops see the drugs aren't prescription. They want to know where they came from.

They find the kid. The kid tells them about you. Do you really want to go down this path?"

"Rose is terminal," June says. "She already has morphine. She knows what she's asking. She's done this before."

Cyril steps around to face her. "Done what before? Tried to off herself?"

"No. Helped her dad."

"Oh, gee, that's a relief."

"She was charged with assisted suicide."

"What the hell?"

"They almost revived him," June says. "That's why she doesn't trust morphine."

"Sweet little Rose killed her dad?"

"No. She just helped him."

Cyril pulls up his own chair and sits in front of June. "Listen, honey, you asked me to go to the dinner party with you because you weren't sure you wanted to be alone with those two. Well, now you know why your spidey senses were tingling. If you want to help Rose, talk to her nutty professor husband. Let him track down the kid."

"She doesn't trust him," June says. "I told you. She thinks he's losing his mind."

"She's dying. Whose mind are you going to trust? The desperate and dying, or the entertainingly loopy?"

"She's right," June says.

Cyril is exasperated. His voice clicks up a pitch. "So, you think the old man is less competent to have this conversation than that pile of sticks I met at dinner? I talked to him in the kitchen and he seemed okay to me. A little random—talking about cannibalistic bugs and PTSD—but he was cooking and talking and doing both reasonably well. I had to step in a couple of times to keep things from getting ugly with the branzino, but he held his own."

"He's not right," June says. "He broke into my house."

Cyril finds an even higher octave. "What? He broke a window? Jimmied a door?"

"Just walked in while I was out. And he walked out with this."

"A pocketknife. How do you know? Did he bring it back and say oops?"

"I found it in his house."

Cyril's eyes widen, his lashes flutter. "So, you broke into *his* house?"

June explains how it all started the night of the dinner party, when she saw the knife on the professor's desk. How when she couldn't find Doug's knife anywhere in her house, she went back to check the one in the professor's office.

Cyril relaxes, regroups. "Okay," he says. "Listen. I don't think that finding—"

"He's not well," June interrupts. "His doctor says its normal, but it's not. He needs help."

Cyril raises his hands in surrender.

"I don't know what to do," June says. "Rose is so sad. Her eyes..."

Cyril cups June's head in his hands. "Listen, sister, I don't care how sad she is or how crazy he is, you need to pull the blinds and shut the Addams Family out of your life. You don't even need your spidey sense to know that nothing good can come of this."

"I know," June says.

"And you're good, Junebug. One of the goodest people I know."

She smiles at her friend. "Thank you, Cyril. That's sweet."

"Can't spot a winter wren at fifty yards to save your life, but you've got goodness to spare."

"I'm surrounded by crazy people," June says.

"Well, there's crazy and then there's cuckoo. Let me girlsplain you the difference."

Cyril continues to joke. June smiles agreeably. But she's not really listening to him. He's letting down the blinds on the Geddes's side of the room and saying something about a bird watching trip he'd like to organize to Estonia. The closed blinds do nothing to shut out the truth.

"I'll be right back," June says, and heads out to check on the boys.

&#8766;

Rose is awakened by the sound of someone coming through the back gate followed by a loud knock on the kitchen door. It takes Kel several minutes to make it up to the bedroom. He's carrying a glass of lemonade. He sets the glass down on her nightstand.

"Rose, dear, there's a boy downstairs. One of Mrs. Danhill's. He says you want to talk to him."

"The one you hired?" Rose asks.

"Yes. He says you asked to see him."

"Send him up."

"Why on earth—"

"I have a gardening request," Rose says.

Kel cocks his head as if trying to figure out what he's missing. "I can pass along any work you'd like—"

"No. I'd like to—discuss it with him. Please."

"Okay," Kel says. "Would you like anything else?"

"Just the boy."

Kel nods meekly and turns to leave. *This is how our eyes betray us*, Rose thinks. *They grant substance to things that have none. My eyes tell me Kel's there filling space between me and the door. His body reflects light, suggesting matter and movement through space, and my mind's eye tells me his body passes through the doorway and turns left down the hall. But I know what my eyes don't. I know there's nothing there at all.*

"Hey, Crypt Mistress," the boy says cheerily. "Never thought I'd see you again. I mean, you know. Anyway, the widow said you want to talk to me."

"Her name is Mrs. Danhill," Rose says. "Show respect."

"Not you too," Joe sneers. "You drag me up here to talk manners? Shee-it."

"No, I did not. You told me—there's better drugs."

Joe's body seems to armor itself involuntarily, arrange its defenses. He glances around the room. "Yeah. So?"

"I want a better drug."

Joe rubs his chin and paces the room. He walks out to the deck and looks over the railing, then returns to the bedroom with one of the café chairs. He goes to Rose's side of the bed, takes a seat, and leans in so he can speak in a hard whisper. "I don't remember saying anything about being able to *get* you drugs. I mean, I know there're better drugs. But, you know, because that's what I've been told."

"Joe, right?" Rose says.

"Yes, ma'am. Some people call me Big because my cousin is Little Joe. I'm thinking about having people call me HB, though, for honey badger. You ever see one? Serious badasses. They kill cobras and—"

"Joe. Stop. Tell me about—the drugs."

"I don't know." He leans toward her. "I mean, you could be some sort of undercover narc trying to get one more bust before you check out—"

"Joe!" Rose leans over so their noses nearly touch. "I don't have time or—patience for this."

He stiffens and sits up, giving himself space. "You're serious."

"As a honey badger," she says.

Joe smiles. His body returns to its fluid state and he leans forward again. "I like that. I like you. What do you want to know?"

"About *better* drugs."

"Well, there's better because they're cheaper, like the white stuff, you know, birdie powder. And then there's better because it takes you places you never want to come back from. That's your apache, China white. Some people like to mix 'em up. Call it TNT."

"Give me the *ology*," Rose says.

Joe smiles again. It's a handsome smile, Rose thinks. A mature smile for such a young man.

"You're funny," he says. "Heroin, fentanyl, or a mix. All three blow away your not-so-mighty mo. You just have to be careful. They're loaded guns. But then you probably know all that *ology* stuff, don't you?"

"How much?" Rose asks.

"There you go again, thinking I can get you this stuff. I mean, I can talk to somebody and maybe—"

"No time, young man. Either help me or—send someone who can."

Joe hesitates. The smile is gone. He's thoughtful now. Calculating.

"Okay," he says. "Which one?"

"Fentanyl."

He doesn't say anything, just looks at Rose, nodding. "How much?"

"More than enough," she says.

Joe sniffs and nods again like he's worked out a problem and says, "Let me see what I can do. Maybe keep a couple hundred dollars around, you know, just in case."

Rose points to Kel's nightstand. "Open that drawer. There's a small cash box."

Joe plucks a couple of tissues from Rose's box and walks around to Kel's side. He uses them on the knob when he opens the drawer. *Clever boy,* Rose thinks.

"Yeah," he says, "there's a box."

"Open it."

Joe fumbles with the slide on the box, trying to open the latch without tearing through the tissues. He manages to lift the lid.

"How much is there?" Rose asks.

"I don't know. Plenty."

"How much do you need?"

"I don't need anything now. I've got no product."

"I trust you," Rose says.

Joe huffs. "You know, that's the first dumb thing I've ever heard you say."

"I trust you," Rose repeats.

He looks at her, his face gravely serious. His honey badger look, she imagines. "Give me one-fifty," he says.

"Take two hundred," Rose counters.

Joe carefully extracts the bills and shuts the lid. He returns to

Rose's side of the bed and searches out her bottle of morphine. Holding up the bottle in his tissues, he asks, "How many of these do you take a day?"

"Depends. Most days three—maybe four."

He nods knowingly, pours a dozen tablets into the lid of her pill tray and holds up the bottle. "I'll bring this back." He pockets the bottle with the rest of the pills, crumples the money into the tissues, and shoves the wad into his pocket too. He pulls more tissues and wipes the back of the chair, keeping the tissues between his hand and the metal arc as he carries it back out to the deck. He goes to the dresser, picks up the Jaguar model, wipes it off, and replaces it. He thoughtfully scans the room. "Give me a few days," he says, and leaves without looking back.

# Honey Badger

*Wednesday, June 3*

Her condition has deteriorated daily. Every time Kelsey lifts the sheet in the morning, she seems somehow frailer. The resurgent strength that spring inspired is slipping away. The strongest part of her is the fusty smell he assumes is the cumulative trapped gases of decay. Each day as they prepare for their morning routine, he's sure he will find new spontaneous bruising, or maybe her feet dipped to a deeper purple, or even, as in his nightmares, a shed limb. She's spending all her time in bed and refusing trips to the deck. Her appetite is not what it was just last week. She shows no interest in finishing the jigsaw puzzle that has occupied one corner of the room since March. He's noticed her latest crosswords are abandoned with blank squares remaining. He hovers more, lingers on the deck reading his paper. He's hoping she'll perk up and ask to join him. He can't decide if she's dying or conserving her energy for their anniversary, just two days away. Resting up for her swan song, maybe.

It's midweek and the boys are back already. Kelsey is washing his car when they arrive. Two of them head for June's back door. The third walks toward Kelsey.

"Hey, Professor, is Mrs. Geddes accepting visitors?"

"Good morning, young man. No school today?"

"First day of summer vacation."

"And we haven't even arrived at the solstice yet," Kelsey says. "Lucky you. What brings you here?"

"Hoping to check in with the missus about the job she had for me."

"What job is that?"

"That's what I'm here to find out."

"I'm not sure what state she's in. I'm going to check on her after I finish the car. You can wait or pick up that chamois and dry while I go ask her."

Joe snatches the chamois hanging on the gate and snaps it in the air.

Kelsey drops his sponge in the bucket of soapy water and picks up the hose. He rinses off the car. "All yours, Joseph."

"HB," the boy says.

Kelsey thinks he's playing a prank. "My memory is not what it once was, but you are difficult to forget, Joe. Shouldn't your initials have a J in there somewhere?"

"Was Joe. Now my friends call me HB. Stands for honey badger."

"Ah, the fierce ratel," Kelsey says. "Quite the moniker to live up to."

"I don't know about all that. Just tell Mrs. G that HB is here."

"So, Rose is a friend?"

"Sure. You too, Professor. One big, happy friendly."

"Friendly. Very clever. HB it is," Kelsey says, and heads for the house.

⤚

Lying in her bed with a spot of late-morning sun pooling on her chest, Rose believes she can sense the blanching heat seep below the surface and dry her from the inside out. She sees herself among the scrub and sand of the high desert, her skin falling away, her bones bleaching. The sun as god. Apollyon. Reaper of what he has sown. Without his perfect proximity, Earth would be barren. But the bastard takes life more greedily than he gives it. Draws life to feed his flame. It's a constant tug of war. When he senses weakness, he pulls harder. He declares himself and dares us to challenge his dominion. It is the fucking fire this time.

Kel appears as if she's conjured him and blocks the sun. He says nothing until he's sure she isn't napping. "Hello," he says, and examines her breakfast dishes. "I don't know why I bother. Once again, you've barely touched your oatmeal."

"It's hardly oatmeal," Rose says.

"No? What would you call it?"

"Gruel."

"Well, now I don't think—"

"And unusual punishment."

Kel smiles. Her insult amuses him.

"And here I thought I'd finally lost you," he says. "But there you are, still my thorny briar Rose. Gruel and unusual punishment. Wonderful. I'm commuting the rest of your sentence." As he places her breakfast dishes on the tray, he says, "I have a request from one HB. He wants to know if you're receiving visitors this morning."

"HB?" Rose asks. Kel is about to clarify, but Rose remembers before he has time to begin. "Ah, of course. Send him up."

Kel nods agreeably, though he seems disappointed, perhaps a little jealous that Rose didn't need his honey badger explanation. *Maybe, I should have played dumb. Let Kel participate.* But hurt feelings don't matter anymore. Truth is, Kel's feelings haven't mattered to her for several days now. There's relief in that. She can't be troubling over how anyone else feels about anything at this point. That is a concern for the living.

The boy enters without announcing himself, walks around the bed, and kneels next to Rose. He brings a red bandana out of his pocket and opens it, revealing her morphine bottle looking like the disk floret of a wilting bloom. She can see a packet of white powder inside the orange plastic.

"This is the 'more than enough' you ordered," he says. "And here's your change." He holds up two twenty-dollar bills.

"Keep it." Rose takes the bottle from him and brings it close to her weary eyes. "It's powder," she says.

"Couldn't get pills."

"How do I take it?"

Joe shrugs. "Most snort or shoot. Guess you could sprinkle it on something."

"How much?"

"Dunno. Never tried to OD. You've built up resistance with the mo, so maybe half that. But your lungs are shot, so maybe less will do it."

"Big help."

"Ask your doc," Joe says, without his signature smile.

They stare at each other, then Rose says, "Thanks."

"It's gotta look like it was the mo," he says. "I'm going to disappear the rest of those pills."

"Not yet."

"Look, I ain't coming back. That mo's gotta go and that baggy and anything left in it too."

"We'll take care of it."

Joe rubs his face nervously. "I don't know," he says.

"Trust me," Rose says.

Joe flashes a skeptical grin. "It's not you you're asking me to trust."

Rose manages a grin of her own. "No, guess not. Maybe you shouldn't come—help out Mrs. Danhill—anymore this week."

Joe nods. "Listen, Crypt Mistress, don't screw this up."

"You should go," she says.

Joe stands up and looks down at her. "I know this is what you want," he says. "Wish I could feel better about it."

Rose's gratitude is but a slight lifting of her cheeks and the deeply cleft corners of her mouth. She hopes it's enough.

"See ya, Mrs. G."

Joe leaves without displaying any of the swagger she has come to expect of him. She wonders if doing something he considers the right thing diminishes him in his own eyes.

# THE EVENING'S LAST SINGER

*Friday, June 5*

Rose sits propped up in her bed waiting for Kel. She inventories the assortment of sensations playing through her body to see if there's anything new she should take heed of, anything that might be trying to signal some oversight in her planning, or perhaps a softening of her resolve. But there's nothing she has not already felt a thousand times and, in many cases, worse. Nothing that betrays hidden doubt.

*Stop gloating, Dad. We both knew it was only a matter of time. This is my time.*

She stares out at the unremarkably beautiful morning. A day like any day. As good a day as any day. Invisible children are bickering. An invisible woodpecker chisels a tree. An invisible car alarm bleats. An invisible dog barks.

Kel creeps into the room with a bouquet of foxgloves and daylilies completely obscuring his face. "*Buon anniversario, principessa!*"

"Oh my," Rose sighs. "They're gorgeous."

"*Come te, amore mio.*"

"Ha," Rose coughs. "Not like me yet—but give them—a few days."

Kel places the vase on Rose's side table and primps the bouquet.

"Did you deliver the—invitation?" she asks.

"I did," Kel says, still arranging the blooms.

"And what did she say?"

"She wasn't home. I left it in her door."

"Hmm," Rose says, considering this wrinkle in her plan. "Is her car there?"

"It is." He finishes with the flowers and turns his attention to Rose. "Her little dog didn't respond to my knocking. I'm guessing they're out for a walk. Not uncommon this time of morning."

"Oh, good." Rose inhales deeply and releases the tension of uncertainty. She is confident she can count on June. She certainly would have said something yesterday if she weren't going to be around today. "Can you believe—I made it?" Rose asks.

Kel brushes a rogue wisp of hair off her forehead. "Yes, you did, and yes, I can. Your will is legendary." He sits on the edge of her bed. "It's our anniversary and I don't know what to make for brunch, and there's so little time left before June will be here. I wish you'd given me a day to prepare."

"It's okay," Rose assures him, and pats the back of his hand. "We'll work out—a simple menu—together."

Kel begins to say something then stops, a word half-formed on his lips trapped behind his teeth. His eyes shift about as if he's tracking an object that's moving at great speed. A fly, Rose guesses, but there isn't one in the room. Now his eyes are scanning her face, now looking off over her shoulder, now back to her and then overhead as if whatever is careening around the room is incorporating her face into its game. His frozen mouth relaxes into an appreciative smile as if to signal that whatever he is watching has either settled or flown off.

"What is it?" she asks.

His eyes resume their journey for several seconds and then flutter to a stop back on her face like a butterfly coming to perch. "Oh, my grandiflora," he says, "if only you could see what I see."

She reaches up and touches his cheek. He nuzzles her hand and closes his eyes.

"I see you," she says.

Kel opens his eyes and says excitedly, "I think I've finished the piece."

"Your article?"

"Yes. Will you read it?"

"Of course. Go get it."

Kel starts to get up but stops himself. "Do we have time?"

"Plenty," Rose says. "And bring ice cream."

He crouches and leans toward her as if she has shared a conspiratorial secret. He glances around the room and whispers in response, "Ice cream before brunch. Do we dare?"

"Do we still have—double dark chocolate?"

"At least half a pint, if memory serves."

"Then we dare."

"Such hedonism. The gods will punish us."

"Yes. But first they will—envy us."

Kel kisses her delicately on the lips and dances his way out of the room in a sort of epileptic stork's version of a cha-cha.

✑

Kelsey is cheered by Rose's playful suggestion. He refuses to let the looming brunch preparations spoil the moment. If Rose says there's time, then time there is. She is the Timekeeper, the Mistress of Moments. On the way to the freezer, he realizes he is humming and tries to identify the tune. Just nonsense, he decides. There's a hint of "Mairzy Doats" in the first bit, but after that nothing he recognizes. It's appropriately jaunty and that is all that matters now. He grabs the ice cream and a single spoon and hums the untune back up the stairs. From his office he collects his printed article, Cyril's book of bird songs, and his resin-entombed Manty. He returns, still humming, to the bedroom.

Proudly displaying his bounty, he says, "Prepare to indulge."

Rose pats the bed. Kelsey puts the papers and paperweight on his side table, tosses the book on the bed and climbs in next to Rose. He pops the lid off the ice cream and is poised to dig in when Rose says, "Wait for it to soften. Give it to me." She sets it on her side table by the flowers. "You brought *Morning Songs*," she says.

"Just in case you get bored with my article," he says. "The birds are infinitely more entertaining."

Rose is smiling. *There it is,* he thinks. *The faint flush of the life still coursing beneath her diaphanous flesh. There's an air of wonder about*

*her. It's as if Dorothy has stepped from her windblown house into Oz.*
"I've missed you," he says.

"Me too," she says, and runs her fingers through his hair. She brings her hand to rest on his cheek and says, "Kel, it's time."

That word again, he thinks. "Time, darling? I thought you said we had plenty."

Her eyes glisten but do not well. It's not sadness that moistens them; it's something he has no word for, a nameless certainty he doesn't recognize.

"Time for me to go," she says.

He hears her. The words are clear, their meaning concise. He has no problem understanding the euphemistic usage. Yet all he can think to say is, "I'm confused. What about our anniversary? Our celebration?"

"I'm sorry," she says. "I planned without you. I didn't want you—talking me out of it."

"Planned?"

Rose picks up the ice cream and pokes at it with the spoon. The edges have softened. The center is still solid. She hands him the container. "Wrap your hands around it," she says. "Warm it up."

He cups his hands around the container and holds it in front of him. "What are we doing?"

She reaches under her blanket and brings out a small plastic bag of white powder. "When it's ready, I'll—put this in. Then I'll celebrate—our anniversary."

"Why would you do that?"

"Because it's time."

"You're leaving me?"

"I am."

"But our brunch."

"Kel, I can't anymore. Can't sit helpless. Can't watch. Too hard. I'm sorry."

"Can't watch? Rose, what are we talking about?"

"You, dear. Can't watch you leave me."

"But I'm not going anywhere. I'm the one watching. Two years now."

"Yes. I've been selfish. Greedy. It's time." Rose reaches for the ice cream.

Kelsey withdraws the container. He realizes he has a say in this after all. He denies her the container and considers its slowly liquifying contents. There was a small family-owned ice cream parlor in Marrsville when they first moved here. The store's name escapes him, but he remembers their diabolical, full-fat dark chocolate with chocolate chunks. Heart of Darkness, they called it. Rose would order a scoop and would not speak until she had licked the last drop from her spoon and tipped the cup to her lips to drink the dregs. The stuff in the container he's holding is a pale approximation of that treat. It is unworthy of her. He pulls it closer to his chest.

"Don't," Rose says, her hand still reaching. "This is my choice."

"Your choice?" he says. "Selfish to your bittersweet end then?"

"Yes. And one day—you'll make yours."

"I made mine. Forty-seven years ago. In sickness and health."

"Now we part," she says. "Please." Her bony fingers beckon.

More out of curiosity than consent, Kelsey relinquishes the container. He watches Rose pour in the powder and stir. She hands him the empty plastic packet. "Flush this and those pills—down the toilet."

Kelsey takes the packet but doesn't move. Rose is looking at him expectantly. "Now?" he asks. Rose nods. He picks up the pill tray on his way to the bathroom and does as directed. When he comes back, Rose is eating the ice cream.

"Thank you," she says, between bites. She savors the next spoonful. With her eyes closed, she turns the spoon upside down and draws it out slowly through pursed lips. She opens her eyes, looks straight into Kelsey's, and she says, "Two solitudes. Thank you for it all. I love you, bug man."

⁊

When June and Jonesy return from their morning walk, there's a powder-blue envelope stuck in her screen door. The preprinted

calligraphic *You're Invited!* on the outside of the envelope gives
away that it's an invitation.

"Someone's having a party," she says. Jonesy looks up with
expectantly wide eyes. June glances around to see if whoever
delivered it is still nearby. There are a couple of kids playing
up the block, but they are not a family who would invite her to
a party. She flips open the unsealed envelope and removes the
card. The printing is familiar from the Post-its tacked up around
their house. She's invited to join Rose and Kelsey Geddes for a
modest celebration of their forty-seventh wedding anniversary.
"That's sweet," she says. Jonesy cocks his head. The invite is
for brunch on the balcony at around eleven. *Let yourself in,* it
says. It's only 10:35. *A little early,* she thinks, *but then Kelsey can
probably use a hand preparing and serving the brunch, no matter how
modest.* She takes a few minutes to get Jonesy settled, packs a
few of Rose's favorite cookies, and makes her way next door.
When she comes through the gate, she announces herself from
the backyard.

"Rose? Kelsey? Hello. I got your invite. I'm on my way up.
I hope I'm not too early."

The kitchen door is open. There's no evidence of any food
preparations for the brunch she's been invited to. She decides
to take the cookies she's brought upstairs, assuming they have
the rest of the food up there already. The house is uncommonly
quiet, like the day she found Doug's pocketknife, only quieter
still because the professor has apparently forgotten to wind the
clock in the living room, leaving it, too, motionless, silent.

"Kelsey?" she calls from the foot of the stairs.

No response. At the top of the stairs she looks into the professor's office. Only papers, books, and his biblical bugs. She
calls out again. Still no response. As she enters the bedroom,
she sees the French doors are open, but the Geddes aren't at
the café table.

"Hello, June," Kelsey says.

He's sitting in his bed propped up by pillows and probing
a container of melting ice cream with a spoon as if searching for something. Beside him, the head of her hospital bed

raised, Rose lies with her mouth gaped in eternal awe. In her lap is *Morning Songs*, opened to the page for the *American Robin: Morning's greeter and the evening's last singer.*

"Oh God, what have I done? Kelsey, I'm so sorry."

"Come in, June. It's all right. Sit here by me." He pats the edge of his bed.

June's heart panics, her chest tightens. "Kelsey, are you okay? Should I call an ambulance?"

"No, thank you. Not necessary."

"What are you doing? What's happening?"

"Dear June, relax. It's already happened. And it was remarkably peaceful."

June's tears stream without warning. She can't tell if they have erupted out of fear or sadness or relief or her feeling of helplessness. She notices the photograph of Rose's father is face down. Her pill tray and the bottle of pain killers are empty. June drops her bag of cookies and her hands come together in prayer. She presses them to her lips and speaks through them. "We need to call someone. We can't leave her like this."

Kelsey looks over at Rose and smiles. June sees an expression of admiration, love. "We should have gone together," he says. "But she was so frail, and I was afraid." He releases the spoon and shifts the ice cream container to his right hand so he can reach out with his left and caress Rose's hand. "She was so brave and it was so fast."

"Kelsey, let me call—"

"She showed me the way," he says. "My *principessa*, my *grandiflora*."

"Oh no," June says, shaking her head slowly, composing herself. "No no no. I don't think this is the way," she says. "Not for you. Think about what Dr. Bernstein said. You're depressed. You're grieving, that's all. You can recover. You have years left, Professor, good years. I can help. You aren't alone. Kelsey?"

He is still looking at Rose when he says, "She didn't tell me about our baby for a long time. She didn't want me to blame the horse. When she did tell me, I was so relieved that she was okay, I didn't even think of the loss. It was never real for me. Not like it was for her." He turns to face June. "But I feel it now, the loss. Of both of them. A childless, doddering old widower. Nothing left for me but days filled with a receding past. All that's left is remembering, and I'm no damn good at that anymore."

He's speaking as calmly and coherently as June has heard in weeks. She is reassured. She closes her eyes, her hands still lifted in prayer. "Don't talk like that. There are still good days ahead. We've had many in just these last few weeks, haven't we? There are more to come. There's so much life left in you. You're just sad."

"Just sad," he says, with a tone she thinks is meant to mock her inability to understand what he's saying. He releases Rose's hand and returns his attention to the liquifying ice cream. He stirs it slowly, observing it as if working toward a particular consistency.

June looks around the room for inspiration, something to draw him out of his meditation. The bedroom is tidy. A bouquet of flowers rests on the side table with Rose's stack of books. No crossword puzzles strewn about. The unfinished jigsaw puzzle is still on the card table. Rose's oxygen tank has been packed up and stowed. On Kelsey's nightstand is the mantis paperweight and a neat stack of papers.

"Your article," she says brightly. "You're still working on it."

Kelsey continues stirring. Without looking up, he says, "It's finished with me."

June reaches for the papers. "May I?"

Kelsey hands her the top sheet, the last page of the article. She reads aloud, "*The male's only available defense is to develop a general aversion to the female's allure, to quell his desire, to deny his sole reason for being. Ha!*"

"Ha!" Kelsey echoes, with great amusement. "An impossibility, my Manty! Read on."

June reads silently, her lips twitching the shapes of the words: *An impossibility, my Manty, and you know this. You know us too well. Just look at you, dancing alone in your invisible room. So sure, so confident. You know I'm watching; I can't avert my eyes from the terrible truth of you. This dance is for me, is it not, my love? You, too, desire. You,*

*too, lust not merely for life but for me. You want. You need. Of all the*
*lost details, this much I remember. You want me. Only me. Dance for me,*
*Manty. Oh, Manty, I remember. Lo ricordo!*

June looks up from the page as Kelsey is lowering the ice cream container from his lips. He plucks a tissue from the box by his bed and wipes the chocolate from the corners of his mouth.

"Professor, what did you do?"

He shrugs. "Made my choice."

June feels the tightness returning to her chest. Her breathing quickens. "I'm going to call an ambulance now."

"Just sit with me for a few more minutes," he says, reaching for her hand. She recoils as if he's contagious.

"Don't do this to me," she says.

"Not to you. For me." His hand remains outstretched, his face pleads. She surrounds his hand with both of hers. "There's no rush," he says. "Here." He reaches with his free hand and picks up *Morning Songs* from Rose's lap. "I had no idea robins have so many song variations. Fifteen sometimes twenty different phrases combined in different ways. Can you imagine? Of course you can. You've probably heard them all. Choose your favorite songbird and play it for me."

June keeps her two-handed grip. "Kelsey, I can't. I have to go—"

"Mrs. Danhill, you've been such a good friend to us these last months." He lays the book in his lap. "I'm sorry we've been such a burden in return."

"Stop. You're not a burden—"

He presses his index finger to his lips. His eyelids blink slowly. "The terror," he says. "It's gone."

"Kelsey, I thought…I'm so confused." She tries to release his hand but he twitches his fingers as if to tighten his grip and she stays.

"Sit. It's fast," Kelsey murmurs. He blinks more heavily now, as if he's trying to keep his eyes open but failing. His grip slacks and he is asleep. She pats his cheek to rouse him.

"Kelsey," she says. His eyes open slightly but he doesn't

respond. His breathing is shallow. There's a low gurgle deep in his chest. She watches his lips slowly transition from pink to blue. His entire body shudders as if suddenly chilled and the gurgling gets louder. She stands. His body jerks and is still. A sigh leaks from him like unformed last words. Foamy spittle oozes from the corner of his mouth. She backs away from the bed. She clasps her hands and rocks in place. *Is he gone? Can I still save him?* She scans the room for a phone. Opens drawers. Checks the dresser. She places her fingers on his wrist. Puts her ear to his chest. Drops to her knees. And stays.

June doesn't know how long she has been kneeling bedside when she finally gets up. She averts her eyes from the Geddes and the paperweight catches her attention. She picks it up, turns it over in her hands as if somewhere in there is the answer. What did he see? She examines the mantis from all its transparent angles. June wipes her eyes. "Poor thing," she says. "You're not dancing. That's not dancing." June speaks to the professor without looking at him. "How could you say that? This isn't dancing."

She is down the stairs and in the Geddes's front yard before realizing she is still gripping the paperweight. She takes it home and sets it on the mantel under her herons, beside her hummingbirds.

She calls Kevin.

"Soon," she says when he asks for a date. "I'm ready for a break from Marrsville."

"Did you ever find Dad's knife?" he asks.

"Long story. I'll tell you when I visit."

"Well, give us plenty of warning. We'll want to plan something special."

"No surprises," she insists.

"You're no fun," he says.

She promises to call back with a date next week and they leave it at that.

She dials 911.

She is sitting on her porch swing waiting. A dozen purple, reblooming irises brighten the strip of grass between hers and the Geddes's house. There is a ruckus in their river birch as a posse of sparrows mobs a blue jay. Across the street, Prince barks impatiently as Alice lights her cigarette before tossing his tennis ball. One house over, on the other side of the wall of twelve-foot arborvitae, she can hear the Stern boy practicing his trombone. His dull, distant notes are overwhelmed by the mechanical sound of church bells marking the hour.

# ACKNOWLEDGMENTS

For the science that informs Professor Geddes's article, I am indebted to the work of three people who actually know what they are talking about. Foremost, Dr. Kate L. Barry's paper "Sexual Deception in a Cannibalistic Mating System? Testing the Femme Fatale Hypothesis," accepted by The Royal Society in November of 2014, and her lecture on "Cannibalism in the False Garden Mantid" available on her website http://www.kate-barry.com/dr-kate-barry. Kent Bailey, Professor Emeritus of Clinical Psychology at Virginia Commonwealth University, whose "warrior hawk" theory is referenced in Kevin Dutton's *The Wisdom of Psychopaths*. That I have referenced these respected scientists' research in no way suggests that they approve of my conflation of their work. Other than a brief email exchange with Dr. Barry, I have had no contact with them about the contents of the fictional paper. I'm confident, however, that if they were to read Professor Geddes's take on the Femme Fatale Hypothesis, they would find it as delusional and scientifically flawed as I intended.

I owe thanks to the mentors who helped me shape and reshape and shape again: Nomi Eve, director of Drexel's StoryLab and MFA programs; the faculty of Cedar Crest College's Pan-European MFA program, who provided wise eyes at various stages of development: Keija Parssinen, Jake Lamar, and Alison Welford, with special thanks to my advisor, Robert Antoni, who embraced this project and encouraged me to expand it; M. Allen Cunningham, writer, publisher, and pal, who read repeatedly and closely, and never failed to make it better; Jessica Hatch for doing exactly what she was paid to do: tell the truth; my Regal House Publishing team, Jaynie Royal and Pam Van Dyk, for believing in the book.

Thank you also to early readers Virginia Warheit, Bill Irwin,

Barbara McLees, and Libby Roth-Katz. A special shout out to Martha Roth-Irwin, who, in addition to being an extraordinary person, is a reliable source of both constructive criticism and unconditional support.

And a final thank you to Beth for everything else.